MYSTERIES ABOUND

A MAGGIE BELLE COZY MYSTERY
BOOK 2

Liz Turner

Contents

Prologue
"Thus with a Kiss, I Die"

He stared down at her. His hand gently brushed her cheek. He believed it was almost warm. A cruel trick of a mind that refused to accept the heart wrenching tragedy that lay unmoving before him. He would almost believe his love asleep, were it not for the small bouquet positioned in her frail hands. Hands that were cold to the touch. The array of flickering candles around her bed provided a façade of warm color on her otherwise pale skin.

His fingers wrapped around hers and he lowered to his knees, the wince of pain stretching across his wrinkled features. The pain was not just from arthritic knees joints being forced to bend, but more because he had been too late. And now his love was dead.

Grief overtook him and he dropped his forehead to her chest, where he sobbed loudly. He could almost imagine her hand stroking his head and provided the comforting touch he so sorely needed from her.

The pain was too immense and the prospect of enduring life without her was too impossible to contemplate. He shook his head, the knowledge of what he needed to do stabbing at his heart like a cold knife thrust into his chest.

A trembling hand withdrew a small vial from his pocket. The liquid contents were clear, providing no sign of the lethal effects that would overtake his body if he had but one sip.

He cast one final, longing look at the sleeping face of his love, as though willing her to open her eyes before he shut his. He then tilted his head back and, in one gulp, swallowed the entire contents of the little bottle.

Pain gripped his throat, and he clasped at his neck in a vain attempt to stop the agony surging through every nerve fiber in his body. He shook slightly before releasing all desire to live and falling limp at his love's side, his hand finding hers with his dying strength.

Because of the dusty pillow her head was resting on, the woman's nose crinkled just before she erupted in a less than delicate sneeze.

Chapter 1
Firing Juliet

"Cut!" an indignant voice screamed. "Magdalene Belle, you just ruined utter magic with your uncontrollable nasal cavity!"

"I'm so sorry! It's these blasted feathers," Maggie sniffed, her nose wrinkling as she threatened to sneeze again.

The dead man groaned as he sat up and pulled his aching knees out from under him. He rubbed them with his hands.

"Any more of this and I might put some actual poison in this vial," he joked, with a blue-eyed wink at Maggie. "You were an irresistible Juliet, by the way."

The dead woman on the bed rolled to the side, looked down at him, and offered an apologetic smile.

"I'm so sorry," she whispered. "You were just excellent, Benedict. Your part quite moved me."

"Juliet!" the shrill voice screeched from across the set. "Do you think I have all day to sit around redoing scenes? We have a production to rehearse. That's it," Barb snapped and threw down her clipboard. "I'm pulling you off as Juliet."

"You can't do that!" an elderly woman with a greasy, grey bun on top of her head shrieked. "Maggie is the best Juliet we've got."

"Hold your tongue, Sylvia, or I'll report all your secret, and highly illegal, cats to Michelle," Barb retorted viciously.

"Well, just wait till Michelle hears about the torture you're inflicting on us with this play. I thought it was supposed to be some 'good old Shakespearean fun,' you called it," another elderly man commented while jabbing one of his walking sticks into the air to emphasize each point.

"I'll have you know, Reginald," Barb began her attack, "that the play was partly Michelle's idea and therefore has her full support!"

There was a wave of shocked murmurs, followed by distraught groans. If the owner of the very roofs over their heads was responsible for the Shakespeare ordeal, then there was no escaping.

"Right," Barb dusted down her front, "where was I. Ah yes. Maggie?"

"Mmm?" Maggie responded.

"You're fired. Demoted to Nurse."

"As you wish, Barb," Maggie replied, trying to hide the dejection she felt.

Romeo struggled to his feet. He had to use the frame of Juliet's make-shift bier to hoist himself up and take on their ferocious director.

"Now hold on a minute," Romeo objected. "How am I supposed to pretend to be so in love that I off myself with some poison, if I don't have a dead Juliet to kill myself over?"

Barb raised an already permanently spiked eyebrow, as a result of her many facelifts. "Don't you worry, Benedict darling," she said with a supercilious grin. "Who better to play the role of Juliet for you than myself?"

Benedict paled visibly and looked as though he would rather drink a gallon of poison before having to woo the likes of Barb. Barbara Bristle in no way fancied Benedict, also known as the local town flirt, but she thought acting as his lover would be sufficient punishment for all the women's hearts he had broken.

Sylvia snorted into her sleeve and even Reginald chuckled at the interesting twist their director had provided.

"How will you possibly direct the play and act a key role?" Benedict demanded through a splutter of desperate words.

"Darling," she stroked a long, red fingernail down the side of his cheek, "I was born for this."

"Here we go," Reginald sighed and rolled his eyes. "I'd better find a chair to rest my weary bones in while you give another one of your ... soliloquys."

"When I was younger," Barb began while practically gliding across the splintered wooden stage, "I lived on a stage not unlike this one. Oh, I would do anything for the thrill of it all over again. The live audience clapping after your final performance..." she described wistfully. "The roses that brushed against your skin as they were thrown your way..."

"Probably because they were overjoyed about her finally getting off the stage," Reggie muttered loud enough for Maggie to hear.

"Now hold up, Barb," Benedict said, plucking up his courage. "I'm not too sure I'm happy about changing my Juliet at this late point in the play."

"*Your* Juliet?" Barb repeated, her eyes slits as she stared him down. "In case you hadn't noticed, they entitled the play Romeo *and* Juliet. The play is not all about you," Barb said while stabbing another nail into his chest. "Just like life here at our retirement villa. Our lives don't revolve around pleasing you. Rather, it's about what pleases the audience, which is why I will be Juliet."

Benedict frowned. He thrived on having people like him, and Barb's clear dismissal pushed him off his game.

"Don't argue on my account," Maggie piped up. "I can't bare these dreadful feathers and I'm sure the play would be far better without me botching up all of Juliet's lines."

"You see," Barb hissed, "Maggie has no passion to be Juliet. I, on the other hand was born to perform this role," she paused to make sure everyone was looking at her. The group of misfit actors watched as Barb dramatically swirled across the stage, grabbing a dagger from the prop table and forcing it into her stomach. She dropped like a limp rag doll, her hand draped across her face.

It took another ten minutes of agonizing groaning and weeping before Barb finally twitched one last time and died.

Relief that it was over swept through the group and Maggie wondered if she could use the temporary distraction of Barb's impromptu "teaching moment" to escape to her little cottage and sip a much-needed cup of tea.

Maggie had just made her way to the edge of the stage when Barb's unmistakable voice summoned her.

"Right, let's do this scene from the top, with the new Juliet. Maggie," Barb called loudly, "please be sure to take a moment to learn from a master."

Maggie sighed and slumped into a chair.

"Perhaps," Sylvia piped up, "we might enjoy your scene more if we could see it in the fresh air and sunlit garden?"

"Excellent idea!" Barb almost sang. "My beauty," she bobbed her permed, purple hair, "is only accentuated even further in natural light."

The cast traipsed outdoors, grateful to see the light of day after several hours of straight rehearsal in the gloomy community hall. Maggie blinked against the bright light of the warm summer afternoon. She closed her eyes and breathed in the fresh air scented with rose, lavender, and lily. She felt immediate relief after the dusty stage and ragged props had attacked her senses.

Maggie, the newest resident of Buttercup Villa, a community for the elderly and retired, caught a thrill every time she stepped out into the central garden and courtyard. Rolling lawns were swallowed up by enormous flowering shrubs and bushes dotted with colors and movement which danced right off a Claude Monet canvas.

"I see you're admiring the flowers again, Miss Maggie," came a friendly voice from behind a delicious orange rose bush. "It's thanks to you, I still have a job here and I'm grateful every day."

"Oh, mention nothing of it, Robert. This place would not survive a day without everything you do," Maggie commended him.

"I see your little stretch of garden is pulling together nicely," Robert observed. "Billy is a hardworking lad."

"He's learning a great deal from you, and I really appreciate you taking the time with him," Maggie replied with a smile.

"Us offenders have to stick together," he mumbled with a wry smile.

"We haven't got all day, Mrs. Belle!" Barb called from the center of the courtyard, drawing all eyes to Maggie.

Maggie excused herself and hurried across the stone path Robert had installed to make it easier for the old folk to traverse over the thick lawns. She looked around the freedom of the garden again, unable to take her eyes off the greenery.

Around the edge of the garden, poking out from between ash and birch trees, were the bricked faces of little thatched cottages that were home to the elderly residents. Maggie adored her little cottage with its own patch of unruly garden for her and Billy to tame. She opened her eyes and looked around, amazed at how quickly the small villa had grown in her the feeling of home.

"Talk about beauty being enhanced by natural lighting," Benedict teased her with a gentle nudge of his elbow.

She frowned at him, mildly annoyed with the fact that he not only flirted with her, but with every single woman he laid his eyes on. She was about to reply when a shrill summons was sounded.

"Benedict, Reggie, stop idling around and bring me that bench. I can't very well pretend to be dead on the grass, now can I?" Barb ordered with a hand strategically placed on her hip.

Reggie looked as though he was imagining Barb pretending to be dead six feet under the grass rather than on a bench. Barb watched obliviously as Benedict and Reggie staggered over under the weight of a solid wooden bench, their combined age being just on a hundred and fifty. She then unashamedly positioned herself on top of it and adopted an expression of tragic death. Maggie swore she even saw Barb reapply lipstick so that she could pucker her hot pink lips at Benedict while they forced him to provide his, "Thus with a kiss I die," concluding line.

"Right, from the top. Paris," she threw at Reggie, "prepare to die and this time I really want you to pretend it has cut you in two."

"Charming," Reggie grumbled. "How come I have to fill all the roles of men who get murdered?"

"It's a tragedy, old chap. Everyone gets murdered," Benedict said with a laugh.

This was not well received by Shakespeare enthusiast Barb who glared up at him from her deathbed. Benedict sighed and embarked on his journey of taking out Paris before finding his beloved Juliet dead.

Fortunately, Benedict did not have to fake his tears for very long because the sprinklers unexpectedly turned on and darted each of them with cold spurts of water.

Barb's squeal turned into a gurgle as she got a face full of water. Robert hurriedly ran to turn off the sprinklers, shouting apologies as he went, but by the time he shut the water off, everyone was relatively drenched.

"Robert!" Barb seethed with black rivers of mascara coursing down her cheeks. "How could you be so careless?"

"In his defense," Maggie interrupted, "Robert was not expecting us all to descend on his garden this afternoon."

Barb accepted this, but continued to glower at Robert all the way back to her cottage.

"Rehearsal is over for the day," Barb shouted over her shoulder. "I can't afford to have any of you catch cold and not be able to perform for the town. See you in the morning."

"For the town?" Maggie gasped. "Did you know about that? I thought this was all for fun."

"It's news to me too," Benedict shook his head.

"I've got a pot of Earl Grey waiting to be brewed and a fresh orange cake in need of samplers, if anyone is interested," Maggie offered.

There was a welcome cheer and Maggie saw smiles emerge on tired faces for the first time that day.

"Robert," Maggie said in a lower tone, "I think you've earned an invitation to our secret tea party, too."

"Whatever for?" Robert asked in complete surprise.

"Let's just say that I know the sprinklers were no accident, and that we have you to thank for the premature end to our rehearsal today," Maggie replied, with a sly smile escaping her rosebud mouth.

"You miss nothing, Miss Maggie," Robert replied with a tip of his hat.

"I won't say a word," Maggie promised him, "lest Barb have you fired for sabotage."

"Thank you. I won't be joining you, as I'm still on duty, but I'll gladly accept a slice of cake when I'm finished with work."

Robert offered a friendly wink before disappearing behind one of his prized rose bushes whistling a merry tune.

Chapter 2
Tea with a Splash of Something Stronger

"I think we should complain to someone higher up," Benedict was saying, his face buried deep in the palms of his hands.

Maggie placed a steaming pot of tea on the tray and brought it over to the coffee table. Benedict snatched at a thick slice of orange cake and dug his fork straight in. Maggie had pegged Benedict as an emotional eater, though he still maintained his strong and healthy figure. There was clearly anxiety broiling under his calm exterior.

"Complain to whom?" Maggie asked.

"Exactly," Sylvia agreed through a mouthful of cake. "Mm, this is absolutely delicious, Maggie. Bake it yourself?"

"Of course," Maggie said with a smile, grateful the cake had served its purpose and distracted her old friends from the woes of being unpaid actors under the oppressive rule of Barb the tyrannical director.

"I mean," Sylvia continued, the cake quickly losing its effect, "who's going to listen to a bunch of old crocks complain about slave labor?"

"I don't even mind the acting that much," Benedict admitted.

"Of course, you don't," Sylvia cut in, "I think you actually enjoy wearing make-up, dressing up and prancing around the stage, waving a sword around."

"It's called a rapier," Benedict corrected her stiffly. "And besides, I can't help that I look rather good in tights."

"Are you out of your mind? You're an eighty-five-year-old man leaping about in stockings and pretending to be a sixteen-year-old kid in love. I've seen the handful of painkillers Sarah forks out after rehearsal each day. You're an old crock just like the rest of us," Sylvia fired at him with a disapproving shake of her head.

Benedict silenced himself by shoving the rest of his cake in his mouth, all the while glaring at Sylvia.

"I'll have you know," he finally muttered, "that I'm only seventy-one."

"More cake?" Maggie offered weakly.

"Sorry Benedict," Sylvia managed between gritted teeth. "It's not really you I'm cross with."

"Why does the play trouble you so much?" A perceptive Maggie asked gently.

"Oh, blast!" Sylvia said while launching herself out of her armchair. "I can't stand taking orders from Barb. Who does she think she is?"

"She is a little over the top," Maggie agreed. "But she's rather likeable otherwise."

Maggie could feel Sylvia's black, beady eyes burning into her.

"Let me make it quite clear that when I decided I would retire in the charming little village of Blooming Hill, surrounded by fields of wildflowers and enormous trees, and then move into the promising home for the elderly called Buttercup Villa, I did not expect to be bossed around and forced to learn a script that barely qualifies as English, all for the absolute pleasure of Barbara Bristle!"

"I'll drink to that," Benedict agreed. He raised his teacup. "Got anything stronger we can put in this?"

Maggie shuffled over to her little drinks cabinet and pulled out a bottle of sherry. She felt they could all do with a healthy glass after the lengthy hours of performance they had forced them to endure.

"The funny thing is," Maggie began, her finger tapping her chin while she thought, "it doesn't exactly seem like Barb is having an absolutely pleasurable time."

"Of course she is," Sylvia barked. She grabbed her generous glass of sherry and perched desperate lips on the brim. "God knew I deserved to be punished for all my wrongs and so he moved Barb Bristle into Buttercup Villa to torment me for the rest of my life."

Benedict giggled like a naughty schoolboy while slurping at his own glass.

"Oh, come now," Maggie chastised her. "Barb looks terribly stressed. I think her hair may even be falling out."

"That's from all the purple dye and perming," Sylvia pointed out.

"All I'm saying," Maggie said while falling gently into her creaking armchair again, "is that there's more to all this than meets the eye."

"Here we go," Benedict said with a smile. "Last week, there was more to it than met the eye when we only received one egg for Sunday community breakfast instead of two."

"And there was certainly more to it when Max took over the vegetable stand in town," Sylvia reminded them.

"I proved quite fairly that Max had his scales unfairly weighted. The town was grateful when I exposed his thieving ways," Maggie replied defensively. "And I do still think there's something going on with the egg shortage at breakfast. Soon we will only get one piece of bacon instead of three."

"Why don't you leave this one alone?" Sylvia suggested. "We've known Barb far longer than you have, so we can take care of this one."

"I just don't understand why a woman bordering on eighty would want to go through the stress of putting on a play for the town? It's going to kill her more than it kills us."

"It's Barb," Benedict explained. "She spent half her life on Broadway and is always desperately trying to claw her way back to her glory days, if they ever truly existed."

"Or so she tells people," Sylvia cut in. "I'm sure she wasn't allowed to boss people around there."

"Anyway," Benedict continued, "I don't want you to worry your pretty head, Maggie dear. You've taken in enough strays without adding Barb to your list."

"Strays?" Maggie repeated with an indignant dip of her chin. "Sylvia's the one with the problem of taking in too many strays."

"I'll have you know I gave away three cats last week, all to loving homes. So, I'm down to eleven."

"Oh really," Maggie said. She folded her arms across her chest and studied Sylvia. "Because I saw you sneak in another one of your baskets full of squirming kittens last Saturday."

Sylvia turned a deep shade of red, which was not a result of her second glass of sherry. "We all have our minor problems. How's your delinquent gardener doing?"

"Don't call him that," Maggie huffed. "Billy is doing well, thank you."

"I like the lad. Unfortunate he tried to rob the pub," Benedict added.

Maggie's introduction to Billy had been on the first day she had set foot in Blooming Hill. Finding herself in the right place at the right time, Maggie had stopped the young man from robbing the local pub of all its cash. A little further digging revealed that one of the scheming pub employees had put an impressionable and desperate Billy up to it. It had not been hard to see that Billy's impoverished home circumstances had pushed him to accept the only helping hand which had been a criminal one.

"I like Billy," Benedict began. "He's a hardworking young man and I'm glad he didn't have to go to prison, thanks to you."

"Yes, it was a good thing that I thought there was more to Billy's case than met the eye. You know, he's almost finished his community service," Maggie informed him. "They discounted him twenty hours because of good behavior."

Sylvia shook her head. "Strays. You attract them. Then there's gardener Robert, who merrily drugged Benedict, and I, disguised himself as someone we knew, and robbed us of a few thousand dollars. I still haven't gotten over that one."

"Again, a man in a desperate situation. By the way, the money you 'gave' him helped cover his wife's treatment, and she is on the mend," Maggie explained.

"All I'm saying," Sylvia interrupted, "is that you see the good in people to a fault. Do not try to turn Barb into another one of your human RSPCA subjects, you hear? Barb will get what's coming to her."

Maggie frowned at her unreasonable friend until the uncomfortable silence was interrupted by a knock on the door. Sarah had arrived.

"I'm sorry I'm a bit late with your afternoon meds, but I was knocking on empty cottage doors only to discover Benedict and Sylvia are here anyway," Sarah huffed, slightly out of breath.

Sarah smiled at them with rosy cheeks. She had scraped her auburn hair up into a scruffy bun, which likely only took her a precious thirty seconds that morning. She wore, as usual, her pale pink scrubs and purple crocks. Without a stitch of make-up or time to look after herself, Sarah was still the epitome of a lady in manners and etiquette.

"Some tea, Sarah dear," Maggie suggested.

"I'll get it myself," Sarah blurted. "Thank you. Oh, and the kids were ever so grateful for the orange cake you sent for after school."

"I'm glad," Maggie replied politely while watching Sylvia mouth the words 'another stray' at her.

"Have you seen Barb this afternoon?" Maggie inquired.

"I did. She looks dreadful. I think this play is going to be the death of her, though you do all look so wonderful up there saying such clever things to each other," Sarah gushed from the kitchen. "You brought me to tears with your concluding speech, Benedict. And your Juliet looked so beautiful."

Sarah dabbed a tissue to her eyes while she stirred her tea, deep in thought. "To be in love," she continued, her mind a million miles away, "must just be so… so…"

"Such a pain when it's Barb Bristle you have to kiss," Benedict spat, interrupting Sarah's fantasy of stage love.

"Barb? I thought Maggie was Juliet!"

"I got fired, I'm afraid," Maggie replied. "Juliet should not be a sneezer."

"I'll have to give you something for your sinuses tonight," Sarah replied, making a note in her little medical book.

"I know what I'll do. I'll go on strike as Romeo until Barb steps down and lets Maggie be Juliet again."

"Oh nonsense," Maggie laughed.

"Well, I'll come up with something," he threatened. "Barb wears so much lipstick. I'm scared I'll get stuck to her if I give her a kiss."

"Benedict!" Sarah scolded him. "It's lipstick, not superglue."

"Sarah, while you're here, there's something I want to talk to you about," Maggie said, taking over the conversation. "Now it's only a matter of small importance, but with very large consequence."

Sarah set the pill canisters aside and gave Maggie her full attention. "Alright, this sounds serious. What is it?"

"Why are we only receiving one egg on a Sunday instead of two?" Maggie asked gravely, her eyes searching Sarah's for the truth.

Benedict and Sylvia erupted with laughter before silencing themselves with their sherry glasses.

"I'd hoped you wouldn't, but I knew you'd notice. It's rather embarrassing, Maggie," Sarah uttered in a low voice, her eyes darting round the room.

"Are there a lack of finances?" Maggie probed further. Even if Sarah did not answer her directly, Maggie could usually find her answer in Sarah's open expressions.

Sarah nodded, her face very serious. "We've had to cut back on a few unnecessary things. The expense of all the renovations here has cost far more than Michelle expected."

Sylvia and Benedict choked on their laughter the moment they realized that, yet again, there really had been 'more to it' than they had thought.

"But all the residents are paying their rent," Maggie reasoned, "so surely that is enough to cover the running costs of the facility?"

"I'm not sure how it all works, Maggie, but cutting back on an egg here and there will not kill anyone and it might mean a lick of fresh paint for the roof. So we go on," Sarah explained.

"I heard we're performing our play for the public. Is the plan to sell tickets so that we can bring some money in for the villa?" Maggie reasoned, all the pieces falling together.

"You're not entirely wrong," Sarah admitted. "Michelle thought Barb's play might make the retirement villa seem more appealing to the public, so not only would we get a few more residents for the empty cottages, but it will raise a little extra cash."

"Hmm," Maggie concluded with a twinkle in her eye. "Seems like there really was more to it than I thought."

"I want whatever pills you're giving her," Sylvia said to Sarah. "I want my brain to work like that, too."

Sarah chuckled. "That's from no pill of mine."

Chapter 3
The Fiery Director

Maggie sank her fork into one of two fried eggs on her plate. She had snuck out of the Villa early that morning to a local café so that she could get a decent breakfast inside of her before tackling another day of dreary rehearsals.

"You've got a healthy appetite this morning," Billy said with a cheery smile. He had stopped on the sidewalk and was waving at Maggie.

"I was hoping I would spot you walking past. Come join me. I've already ordered you a breakfast. They're keeping it warm in the kitchen."

"You shouldn't have, Ms. Maggie," Billy said, attempting to reject the mouthwatering offer. "I've already eaten."

Maggie took one look at the young man's hungry eyes and knew he was lying. Billy's father had died young, leaving Billy's mother to raise five children. Her own health did not allow her to work, and so providing for the family had largely fallen on the eldest, Billy. There were no lavish breakfasts with one egg, let alone two.

"No arguing. Come and sit."

Billy complied, though he complained he would be late for work.

"It's hardly a crime when your boss is the one making you late," Maggie chuckled. She signaled to the waitress, and Billy's breakfast arrived after a couple of minutes.

Billy looked down, his eyes unblinking, at the eggs, sausages, beans, bacon, potatoes, and toast with jam on the side. Next came a small pot of black coffee.

"Thank you, Milly," Maggie said, despite the sneer Milly wore on her face while serving Billy. "Is there a problem?"

"It's not in our habit to serve criminals breakfast here, ma'am," Milly retorted, her bulgy eyes fixed on Billy.

Maggie did not like confrontation. It was not in her nature to stand up to people or tell them they were being small.

"Then I think we shall take our business elsewhere," Maggie stated simply, a slight quaver in her voice.

It upset her that society could be so closed-minded, quick to latch onto any rumor, or fleeting fragment of gossip that passed their way. For some reason, people enjoyed being united through a common hatred or fear.

"Is there a problem here?" a deep voice inquired from behind Maggie.

While she could not see the owner of the voice, Maggie could tell he carried a certain amount of authority, for he spoke pointedly and without fear of being overheard.

The waitress squeaked and shook her head. "No, of course not, Sheriff. I was just concerned about what the public might think if they saw us serving..." she flicked a look at the back of Billy's head.

"Serving...?" the Sheriff repeated, clearly waiting for her to complete her thought.

The young woman turned blood red, and she mouthed the word 'criminal' to the sheriff.

"My dear girl," he said gently but firmly as he walked around the table and into Maggie's line of sight, "Billy is no criminal. He helped us put a very dangerous man behind bars who had every intent of hitting up all the businesses in Blooming Hill, including this one. So, you should serve his breakfast on the house, along with absolute gratitude. Now, bring me a coffee, please."

The woman curtseyed awkwardly and sprinted away, nearly knocking over a cupcake stand.

"Good morning, Billy," the tall officer loomed into view and extended a firm hand for Billy to shake, the muscles flexing as he provided an extra tight squeeze. "Nice to see you're making friends in our small town."

Billy held his grip without wincing. "This is Ms. Maggie Belle. She's the lady I told you about that offered me a part-time job working in her garden."

The Sheriff turned cool, grey eyes on her and surveyed her for a second. She could see the cogs effortlessly whirring in his brain while he put together all the pieces of information he had received that contained her name.

"Ah," he said with a twitch of his thick, black and grey mustache. "Now that is a familiar name around the station. I thought I recognized you from the pictures. Didn't you bring a couple of your friends in, claiming that money had been stolen out of their bank accounts? My boys said you gave them quite a hard time."

"That would be me," Maggie admitted with a weak smile, wondering if there was a mug shot of her pinned up on a board somewhere in the police station.

"Did your friends ever find their money?"

She could hardly explain that the local gardener had been the thief and, instead of handing him over to the police, they had taken justice into their own hands by gaining a confession, accepting signs of visible repentance, and moving on with life like one big, happy, dysfunctional family.

"Yes, we tracked down the missing money," Maggie replied carefully. "It's lovely to meet you, Sheriff. I believe you're Sarah Duncan's father."

Warmth entered his cold eyes and his lips lost hold of the straight-lined grimace he had been holding. She thought he formed an almost smile. He looked like a different man when he smiled, though his fiercely pressed uniform with polished buttons and shiny badge still reminded them of his formidable reputation as a representative of the law.

"The name is Cedric Duncan. You're the same Maggie as my Sarah's Maggie, then?" he said in surprise, his tone softer. "Sarah mentions you often. So do her kids. Apparently, you make an excellent cake and tell them detective stories."

The bumbling waitress arrived with a coffee, which she was not sure where to set down. Maggie invited the sheriff to join her table and, once he agreed, the waitress set down his coffee and fled.

"Nervous girl," Cedric remarked. "Tell me, Mrs. Belle, are you happy in Blooming Hill?"

"Very," Maggie replied eagerly. "I miss my daughter, of course, but she's finally happily married and occupied with her husband."

"And you don't find your retirement a little... boring?"

"No, I have plenty to do, really. At the moment, our Villa is putting on a performance of Shakespeare's *Romeo and Juliet.* You should come see it," Maggie said with a smile.

The sheriff raised an eyebrow, and she watched as his mustache disappeared behind his coffee mug.

"I'm glad your time is well-filled then," Cedric continued. "I was a little worried that you might be one of those interfering old ladies who finds entertainment elsewhere."

"And where might that be, exactly?" Maggie asked, while pushing her plate aside. She had a feeling she knew where the sheriff was heading.

"Now and then we get one of those meddling women who believe they're the next Sherlock Holmes and they pry into police business."

Billy shot Maggie a look. He hid an amused smile behind his sleeve before continuing to scoff down his breakfast.

"I would never dream of interfering in police business," Maggie insisted sincerely.

"Excellent," he grinned at her, his mustache widening across his face. "I was a little concerned when I started hearing rumors about an old woman at Buttercup Villa who could investigate far better than the police ever could."

"Who would say such a thing?" Maggie said after gasping in shock. "I have only heard the most respectable comments about our local police station."

Maggie was not lying, though the comments had all been from Sarah and were about her father, mostly.

"Ah, you flatter us. Well, I'm glad we're on the same page, Mrs. Belle. I would hate for our investigations to be held up because an untrained professional got in the way." The sheriff drained his mug and stood up. "Right, well, I had best see myself to the station. We have a full day ahead of us."

"A pleasure to meet you, Sheriff Duncan."

"Magdalene Belle! Where have you been, woman?" Barb demanded. "Rehearsals were supposed to begin an hour ago!"

Barb was wearing a long, flowing dress that swished in time to her every movement. Her purple hair was wilder than ever, and Maggie found the stage make-up Barb wore daily was quite intimidating when her piercing blue eyes were boring into her.

"Oh, I must have lost track of time," Maggie apologized. "Forgive me, Barb."

"You can hand out everyone's scripts for punishment," Barb ordered.

Maggie could feel all eyes on her. Sylvia was grinning with delight, as though she was pleased Barb was on someone else's case instead of her own. Barb was at the front of the group, instructing her cast of actors on how to speak more clearly when on stage.

Maggie hobbled over to the stack of scripts behind Barb, brushing past Reginald before moving in the opposite direction. Maggie's legs were tired after the walk back from town. As she shuffled on the old wooden floorboards of the community hall, her ankle caught on something, and she lost her balance.

Maggie went down with a screech, her hands instinctively flailing out in front of her to catch onto the table which held the scripts. While she lost no more teeth or risk a broken hip crashing to the floor, she bumped the table, causing a gasoline lamp to knock over.

Benedict was soon at her elbow, helping her back to stable ground again, his hands supporting her as he lifted her up gently.

"It's not like you to be clumsy," he observed. "Luckily, this time, your Romeo was able to save you."

Maggie giggled. But the humor was short lived as a high-pitched scream echoed through the dusty community hall. The smell of smoke pierced Maggie's nose, and she turned back to the table with utter dread. To her horror, the neat pile of scripts was a crackling heap of fire.

The next few minutes were ones of absolute chaos. Screams filled the air, mostly from Barb. Others frantically tried to fan the fire out, which only spurned the flames on more rapidly. Finally, Robert ran in with a bucket of water and stopped the fire in its tracks. Barb then sobbed mournfully over her beautifully copied scripts she had prepared so that the group could learn a few more scenes to include in the play. She threw herself on the table of singed papers and blackened water, wailing loudly.

"Barb, I'm so sorry!" Maggie apologized timidly, her mind reeling from the unfortunate series of events that had befallen her in a matter of seconds.

Barb pulled away from the table, her pink cheeks streaked with black stripes of mascara. Maggie thought Barb looked as though she was going to reach out and strangle her, when she noticed something odd about Barb's sleeve.

"Oh no," Maggie gasped.

"Fire!" Reginald shouted again.

Barb whirled round to see where the source of the second fire was, only to discover that she was it. A cinder from one script had sought fuel in her highly flammable dress. Maggie acted quickly this time, pushing Barb over and rolling her around on the dusty floor to try to stamp out the flames, which lapped like tongues all around the grunting woman. Robert did the trick with a second bucket of water.

A drenched Barb lay sprawled on the floor, her beautiful dress in rags around her. To Maggie's relief, Barb was unharmed physically, not suffering so much as a single burn, though the injury to her pride had clearly been severe.

"I thought," Barb began through gritted teeth, "that you were on my side, Maggie. But I'm thinking you're out to get me because I've taken your cherished role as Juliet."

"No," Maggie laughed desperately. "I would never do that, Barb. I'm happy for you to play Juliet. You've got the brain for remembering lines –"

"First your sinuses ruin the role of Juliet, and now your clumsy feet have cost us a small fortune in photocopies. I'm very disappointed in you!" Barb concluded with a tearful whimper. "Rehearsal over!" she shouted in a wobbly voice before fleeing the hall and disappearing into the safety of her cottage.

Maggie spun round, unable to believe how much had gone disastrously wrong in a matter of seconds.

"Accidents happen," Benedict said with comfort. "Don't think too much about it."

Maggie stared at the scene of the fire. She tilted her head, spotting a piece of threat tied to the leg of the table the scripts had been on.

Benedict was tugging her by the arm. "Let's get out of here," he was saying. "I think I'll cook us some lunch today. Shrimp and potatoes?"

"Sounds delicious," Maggie replied vaguely, though her mind was lost in thought.

"What happened here?" Sylvia gasped as she came bustling in with an armful of costumes.

"You missed all the action, Sylvs," Benedict informed her. "Maggie took a bit of a tumble and set all the scripts on fire."

"Maggie!" Sylvia sang her name as though it was the chorus in an opera. "You did that for me, old girl. How can I ever thank you? This is the best news ever!"

"I did not do that on purpose!" Maggie protested, recalling Sylvia's threat from the day before to burn all the scripts so that Barb could not tell her what to do. "And where were you when all the excitement happened?"

"I was fixing up the costumes. Michelle sourced these from the town-hall costume room, so some of them are threadbare and in desperate need of repair."

"Come on, everyone, no point dwelling on the past," Benedict ushered them out. "Not when there's a delicious lunch awaiting us."

As Maggie was pulled away, she could not help but think that there was definitely more to it than met the eye.

Chapter 4
Two Romeos

Maggie had just set the kettle on when there was a familiar tap on her front door. Sarah piled in with two giggling children running in between her legs.

"Now settle down," Sarah scolded them in a whisper. "Maggie needs her rest, and you'll disturb her."

"Alright," Maggie said with a wave of her hand. "It's nice to have a little noise in here. It beats the long, quiet nights."

"Shall I put a pot of tea on?"

"Already done. I'd hoped you'd stop by after your shift."

"I'm that predictable, am I?" Sarah sighed.

"Not at all," Maggie reassured her. "I wanted to talk to you about something rather confidential."

"Oh," Sarah raised an eyebrow and pulled up a chair.

"It's about the fire today," Maggie began.

"Ah, my dear friend, these things happen. No one was hurt. I checked on Barb myself, and apart from her ego, which went up in flames, she's absolutely fine."

"That's a relief, but I'm afraid that's not it. I just have this off feeling that they set me up."

"Set up?" Sarah repeated, her expression frozen.

"On my way to fetch the scripts, I tripped and knocked over the lamp. The thing is, I saw a piece of string tied to the table leg and I wonder if my tripping was deliberate. What if someone had tied it carefully across my path? The fire and water caused quite a mess, but why else would there be string tied to a table leg?"

"I don't know," Sarah replied doubtfully. "Though honestly, Maggie. Most of the furniture in this place is quite ancient. That string could've been there for years."

"Then there's the lamp itself. Why was it already lit if we hadn't started rehearsing yet?"

"Maybe Barb wanted it as a prop for one of the nighttime scenes," Sarah suggested.

"We always use the lamp unlit in rehearsals. Thinking back, I'm fairly sure I could smell the lighter fluid used in the lamp. It was rather strong around the whole table, though I can't say I saw any on the scripts themselves."

"Someone likely filled it for rehearsal. You know how organized Barb is when she's telling other people what to do."

"Hmm," Maggie mumbled, while tapping her finger to her chin.

"I think you're reading into all of this too deeply. It really sounds like an accident to me."

"Except," Maggie said, settling her gaze on Sarah. "Sylvia told me yesterday that she wanted to set the scripts on fire so Barb would cancel the play."

"Sylvia said that? It sounds like her. She hates taking orders from Barb. But I doubt she meant it, Mags. I mean, gosh, we all say things in the heat of the moment, like, for example, if the two of you don't stop flicking channels on that TV, I'm going to warm both your bottoms!"

Maggie hid her smile and watched as the kids obediently set the remote down on the table and retreat to the safety of Maggie's bookcase.

"Besides," Sarah piped up again, "Sylvia couldn't have done it. She was with me all day, stitching up costumes. She didn't leave my sight until after the fire."

Maggie's eyebrows shot up. She had not expected Sylvia to have an alibi.

"Just as well I didn't confront her. I must imagine it all then," she concluded. "Now, tell me about you."

"Me?" Sarah snorted and then blushed. She flicked a strand of hair out of her eyes and adjusted her shirt.

"Yes, there's obviously something on your mind," Maggie pointed out. "Otherwise, you wouldn't be here."

Sarah sighed and studied her feet for a while. "I love my kids, but gosh, it would be amazing to have a partner again. Single parenting is hard!"

"Yes, it must be very difficult," Maggie sympathized. "But you've raised two such wonderful children."

"I just want someone to share life with," Sarah admitted. "The nights are so lonely I find myself not wanting to go home. I see it in my father too, since my mom died. We're not meant to be alone, Maggie."

"I felt that way after my husband passed away. I didn't know what to do with myself."

"Exactly," Sarah sighed and slumped back into her chair. "I feel a right fool for always choosing badly. Which is why I've done something drastic."

"Oh dear, I don't like the sound of that."

"I've accepted a blind date with one of Benedict's contacts."

"Benedict!" Maggie gasped. "Oh, no, Sarah, what if you end up with a town flirt like Benedict?"

"Benedict is a genuine gentleman beneath it all," Sarah laughed. "How bad can it be?"

"I can tell you how bad it can be. You can end up," Maggie dropped her voice so the kids would not overhear her, "chopped up into a hundred pieces and stashed in someone's freezer."

"You watch too many murder mysteries," Sarah reminded her. "Blind dates aren't all that bad."

"You know what really helped me fight the single blues? Gardening, or knitting, or baking, and a whole score of other hobbies I learned to pick up."

Sarah giggled. "I don't think I have enough strength of character to stand on my own. I'm not like you, Maggie."

Maggie leaned forward and patted Sarah's hand. "You do whatever you think is best."

"Thanks, Maggie."

Sarah checked her watch and told the kids to pack up and get ready to go.

"I asked Dad to pick us up. We're having dinner with him tonight. I hope you don't mind that I asked him to fetch us from here?"

There was an official sounding knock on the door. Sarah opened the door and welcomed her uniformed father inside. When he saw Maggie struggling out of her chair, he raised an eyebrow but said nothing.

"Dad, this is Magdalene Belle, the woman I was telling you about. She's been an awfully good friend to me," Sarah began the polite introductions.

"Twice in one day, sheriff," Maggie greeted him with a handshake. "A cup of tea before you go?"

"No, no thanks," he replied hurriedly.

"Wait, you've already met?" Sarah gasped.

"This morning," her father replied, clearing his throat. "At the café. I bumped into Maggie having breakfast."

"Your father stepped in to defend Billy. The waitress was refusing to serve him," Maggie explained. She handed Cedric a teacup, which looked dwarfed in his enormous hand.

"Yes, small-town matters. Silly, really," he said, his words lost in his mustache.

Sarah beamed with pride at her father. It was clear she wanted Maggie and Cedric to get on well.

"It was sheer chance. I was approaching Mrs. Belle to discuss not meddling in police affairs when I overheard the conversation with the waitress," Cedric added, gaining confidence.

Maggie studied her slippers. Cedric's smile faded quickly when he saw his daughter's expression change. Cedric sipped at his tea awkwardly and did his best to avoid eye contact with Sarah while she delivered a one-eyebrow-raised-stare of disapproval.

"I can't believe you!" Sarah reprimanded her father, not the slightest intimidated by his towering presence. "Maggie has been nothing but a friend to everyone in this town, helping them with matters that the police certainly don't see as important enough."

"Now, Sarah darling, hold on a moment-" Cedric spluttered.

"I mean honestly, harassing an old woman while she's eating her breakfast just because you feel threatened that someone is solving more cases than you are!" Sarah continued, her arms flinging to her hips as she lectured him.

"It's alright, Sarah dear," Maggie came to the sheriff's rescue. "No harm was meant, and no offense was taken."

Cedric hurriedly drained his cup and smacked it down on the countertop. Maggie thought the scalding tea must have burnt the whole way down, though his visible discomfort was more because of being embarrassed by his daughter.

"Dinner, shall we?" Cedric asked before Sarah could reproach him any further.

"Yes, let's get going then," Sarah agreed. She gathered her kids' things and then paused just before the door. "Maggie?"

"Yes, dear?"

"Why not join us?"

Cedric looked as though he had swallowed a toad, but he kept his mouth shut for fear of further reproof.

"No, thank you, Sarah. That's terribly kind of you both, but I think I need a night in. Barb has a big rehearsal day tomorrow."

"Ah, yes, you mentioned *Romeo and Juliet* this morning," Cedric said wistfully. "Not my most favorite Shakespearean play..." he drifted off as though his mind was elsewhere. Then he unexpectantly broke out in the gentlest of voices, his eyes settling on Maggie.

"It is the east, and Juliet is the sun.

Arise, fair sun, and kill the envious moon,

Who is already sick and pale with grief?

That thou, her maid, art far more fair than she..."

"Bravo," Maggie clapped, absolutely stunned by the change in the complex character of Cedric Duncan. "Very well recited, sheriff."

Sarah stood with her mouth agape while her children giggled and clapped.

Cedric seemed to pull back to his senses. His cheeks flushed rosy pink, and he shot out the front door with a half-goodbye, disappearing into the thicket of his mustache.

Chapter 5
"In Fair Verona"

"Abominable, absolutely abominable," Reggie spat while holding up white stockings and a pair of pale purple puffy shorts.

"Reginald, all the men in Shakespeare's time wore tights. It's authentic," Barb replied primly. "You can't be the only male in slacks. It simply won't do."

"I think it's positively indecent!" Reginald ranted with a stamp of his cane. "An old man like me forced to wriggle his creaky body into tights."

"We're not changing your costume and that's final."

Reginald growled and hobbled off, his two walking sticks thumping on the old stage floor as he went. Barb turned her eagle-eyed attention on Maggie. Maggie's brush froze midair, and she turned to face Barb.

"Magdalene, I really did not know you were such an artist," Barb pointed out with surprising positivity.

Maggie felt relief wash over her. She lowered her brush and stepped away from the back wall of the stage to give herself an overall view of her progress. It was an enormous cityscape of Shakespeare's Verona, with the iconic river sweeping through it.

"Thank you, Barb," Maggie said. "It's been years since I've painted a backdrop. I used to do it for my daughter's school every year with their school play, but I'm certainly rusty."

"I agree. I can see some of your lines are shaky," Barb commented with a frown, "but I suppose that's to be expected with a little retirement village play like ours. I have to keep reminding myself that this isn't Broadway."

Maggie looked beyond the subtle insult and at the woman with dark rings under her eyes.

"Are you sure you're okay with managing all this?" Maggie asked in a low voice. "You know, we could postpone the play or put it on hold until you've rested up a little."

Barb turned the same color as her hair, and she glared at Maggie while spluttering incoherent words.

"Put the play on hold!" Barb hissed. "Are you out of your mind? After I've worked so hard!"

Maggie signaled over Mia, the young nurse on duty, who was coyly chatting up Benedict in the corner, to come and assist Barb before she had an aneurism.

"Calm down, Mrs. Bristle," Mia instructed her. "Have one of your pills to settle your nerves."

Billy approached, wet paintbrush in hand, to see what all the commotion was about. He had green paint smeared across the front of his white t-shirt, since he had been helping Maggie with the top part of her mural.

"Looking handsome as ever, Billy," Barb teased with a stroke of a long fingernail down his cheek. "Perhaps you should play Romeo instead of old Benedict. I could do with some fresh blood on this cast."

"Come along, Mrs. Bristle," Mia hurried the old woman away.

"He's underage!" Maggie called after Barb.

"Technically, I'm not underage anymore," Billy corrected her, "though don't tell Barb that. I turned eighteen last week. And my sister pointed out that it's high time I come home with a girlfriend for a change."

"You, a girlfriend?" Maggie chuckled. "Well, have you got your eye on anyone, then?"

Billy dropped his head and smiled. He took up painting next to Maggie so that they could continue their conversation in lower tones.

"Now, don't you go blabbing to all your friends around here," he began with a furtive glance around him.

"I wouldn't dream of it," Maggie assured him, while dabbing her brush into some bougainvillea-colored pink so she could complete the pot of flowers she had been working on.

"There might be a lady I fancy," he admitted.

"There's nothing wrong with that, Billy," Maggie assured him. "You're a nice young man. Clever and hardworking. Any girl would be lucky to have you."

"So, you think I should just come out and tell her I like her?"

"That's always a difficult one," Maggie explained. "Do you tell her outright or take a subtler route and send her flowers first? Depends on the girl, I suppose."

Billy was on his hands and knees, applying green grass in the foreground. "What would you prefer?"

"Oh, my Nicolas brought me flowers," Maggie fondly recalled. "Not expensive shop bought ones like all the other boys. No, he picked a bunch from the fields around our town. Poppies and bluebells. I knew right then that he would very well win my heart if that was what he wanted."

"I wish I could've met him," Billy replied wistfully. "He must have been a real good man to have won your favor."

"He was far better than I deserved. Anyway, enough about me." Maggie shook her head. "Stories about the living are far more exciting. Now tell me about this young lady you're interested in."

"Well," Billy hesitated and blushed slightly, "she loves helping people. She's really caring and looks after others. And I think she's just beautiful."

"She sounds like a gem," Maggie said approvingly. She pretended to turn around to change the color of her paint, but instead she glanced around at the assembled actors, trying to find the young nurse Mia and see her through Billy's eyes instead of her own.

"Is she your age?" Maggie asked, wanting to confirm her suspicions.

"Nah," Billy snorted. "She's a little older than me. But I like older girls."

"Well, that's certainly true, since you spend most of your mornings with me. Do I know her?"

Billy snorted. "You do, actually, but don't go do any investigating just yet."

Mia was a few years older than Billy. Maggie had noticed that whenever Billy was working in her garden, Mia took the time to stop by and check on her, which she would not normally do if Billy was not at work. She had wondered if the glamorous, skillfully make-upped, and perfectly dyed blonde hair of Mia might tempt him in.

Billy was rambling on about what he looked for in a girl when Maggie turned back to her section of the wall. Instead of finding a beautifully painted pot of bougainvillea, Maggie found her flowers disappearing under long streaks of red.

"What's going on?" Maggie asked, astounded by the phenomena.

She stepped away, gasping as parts of her creation vanished under a viscous layer that trickled down from the top. Billy shouted in surprise as his painted grass was smothered in a downpour of what looked like blood. He swiped a finger at the wall and sniffed at it to make sure that it was only paint and not something more ominous.

Billy and Maggie hurried to the base of the wall they were painting and looked up, hoping to glimpse whoever was sabotaging their backdrop, but there was no one in sight.

"Wait here," Billy ordered, before he dashed up the stage stairs and rattled his way up to the top of the wall.

His head appeared over the wall. "No one here, Ms. Maggie," he shouted. "Just a couple of big, empty buckets of paint. Still wet."

Maggie was in shock. But that was nothing compared to the terrifying shriek that ripped through the stagnant air.

"What have you done?" Barb screamed at her. "The backdrop was absolutely perfect! Nothing like I'd ever seen on Broadway before, and you've ruined it!"

Mia was soon at Barb's arm, attempting to calm her.

"It wasn't us," Billy explained. "Someone else destroyed it."

"Why would anyone destroy a backdrop?" Maggie muttered half to herself.

"Perhaps it was the same person who destroyed the scripts," Barb snarled at Maggie, her intent clear.

"Maggie couldn't have been the one who poured the paint," Billy stated firmly. "She was down here on the floor with me, and the paint came from up there."

"Maggie's one of the clever ones. I wouldn't put it past her to rig up some contraption to destroy my play," Barb hissed at her.

"In case you hadn't noticed, Barb, but I'm the one who spent long hours on this painting. Why would I destroy my own work?" Maggie retorted with some bite in her voice. She was tiring of being pushed around by Barb.

Red paint had pooled on the wooden floorboards around their feet, ruining Barb's shoes.

"Just get this mess cleaned up so that we can carry on with the dress rehearsal. Mia, move all the costumes out of harm's way. We don't want any paint splashing on them."

"Alright," Mia complied with a worried expression tainting her barbie doll features.

"Everyone take lunch. We'll be back here this afternoon for a full-dress rehearsal," Barb ordered the cast. "And Maggie," the director rounded on her, "get this mural fixed up immediately."

Maggie sighed and slumped into a chair. She knew that there were several people on the cast who wanted the play to stop, but it hurt her to think that they would use her masterpiece as another thing to destroy so that they could get to Barb.

"Why would they do such a thing to me?" Maggie asked, her voice quivering.

Billy wrapped an arm around her frail shoulders. "Why don't you get home for some tea, and I'll clean this mess up. I'll even work afternoons so that we can paint over the ruined parts. It'll probably turn out even better than the first one."

"I've already taken up too much of your time with this," Maggie replied sadly. "You've got your own life. Girls to chase after. Family to be with. Don't worry about me and my silly problems."

Billy took her gently by the elbow and led her out of the dusty hall and to her cottage, where Sarah quickly descended and brewed a much-needed cup of tea. Maggie noticed that none of her other friends dared stop by. Guilt was the great divider.

Chapter 6
Crime Against Fashion

The atmosphere at rehearsals was rather grim that afternoon. Standing tall behind them was the spoiled cityscape of Verona, covered in blood-red stripes, which Maggie had thought was rather prophetic of the play itself. Maggie watched as her fellow cast members shot nervous glances over their shoulders at the spilled red paint. She wondered if it was guilt that tainted their smiles, or if it was simply the fear of being caught appearing too happy on stage by Barb. Barb insisted her actors were to portray a level of miserableness suitable for characters in a tragedy.

"While our minor production has suffered a few unexpected setbacks," Barb began, refusing to look at the stained mural behind her, "nothing will stop the show from going on!" She punched a fist into the air by a show of mock enthusiasm, but the crowd groaned more than cheered. "Anyway, our costumes have finally been adjusted to your measurements and we wait in anticipation to see what we all look like as a costumed cast. So, without further ado, find the costume bag with your name pinned to the front and promptly get changed."

The group reluctantly swiped through plastic bags attached to hangers until their name popped up, before shuffling off to various restrooms or corners where they would not be seen changing. They had downgraded Maggie to Nurse and so Sarah had to strap on several layers of padding so that Maggie would look the hefty part. She felt a wave of despondence settle on her as she viewed her tiny face smothered inside an enormous costume.

"Well, it doesn't get much worse than this," Maggie sighed. "And I really was trying to make the play a success for Barb. Not much good that did me."

"Cheer up, Maggie," Sarah crooned at her. "You look fantastic no matter what you're wearing. You're still drop dead gorgeous, regardless of your age. And no hideous nun costume could hide that."

Maggie raised a disbelieving eyebrow, which was swallowed up by a hat too large for her head.

Sarah suppressed a giggle. "You'll see. There's a bright side to everything."

"Yes, I'm sure if I walked past the snacks table you set up, I could hide an entire pack of donuts under here and quietly scoff them while all the other more interesting characters get to say their lines," Maggie joked.

"I'm afraid not. Michelle cut donuts from the budget. There are some chopped up carrot sticks though," Sarah offered through compensation.

Maggie's forced smile faded, and she sighed deeply, trying to swallow down the disappointment of not having even a pathetic donut break to look forward to.

A scream echoed from another part of the hall. It was the kind of scream that announced trouble, more than pain.

"Guess someone else found out about the donut cut," Maggie muttered under her breath.

Another indignant shout met their ears.

"Something's wrong," Sarah pointed out, her eyes wide and panicked.

"That sounded like Benedict," Maggie noted. She hoisted up the length of her skirt and pushed her way out of the bathroom door, knocking Mia over.

"Sorry, love," Maggie called down to Mia, who had rebounded off Maggie's rather large midriff and landed on the floor in a blonde heap and tangle of legs.

Sarah and Maggie each grabbed an arm and pulled Mia upright.

"What's all the screaming about?" Maggie asked, her voice muffled by all the fabric surrounding her head.

"The costumes!" Mia huffed, out of breath and pale. "Something really strange is going on, Ms. Maggie. You'd better come and look for yourself."

Maggie forced her way forward, though carrying all the extra cushioning took up much of her precious energy. By the time she reached the stage, she was hot, sweating and out of breath. Black spots swam in front of her vision and she had to find a chair to lean on.

Barb gasped, threw her hand to her forehead, and wailed as though in utter agony.

"Even Nurse's costume is ruined! You look absolutely dreadful, Maggie," Barb groaned while Benedict tried to support her, his hands working desperately to avoid touching too much of Barb's writhing body.

"My costume?" Maggie inquired while giving herself a once over. "There was nothing wrong with mine. This is just what it looks like."

Barb cracked open an eye. "Oh," she said, dropping the performance immediately. "Well, at least yours and Juliet's were spared then. But look at everyone else!"

Maggie cast a glance around the assembled misfit cast, wearing ragged stockings and shredded costumes. Benedict was bordering on the line of public indecency, as they had slashed his stockings all the way up the legs, though his rather tight puffy shorts were still intact. Lady Capulet, Sylvia, was draped in a holey garment, which looked less like a wealthy woman's dress, and more like a homeless person's blanket. Most costumes had either a sleeve or a leg cut off. Maggie assumed her costume had looked bad enough and so the culprit had left it alone.

"I can't wear this, I'm afraid," Reginald was complaining again. "I'd almost come around to the idea of male tights, but now that they're all tattered and holey, I don't think I'd like to put my pale, hairy legs of display for the whole town to whoop at."

Maggie frowned slightly. Reginald had been the one complaining earlier that day when he had seen his completed costume.

"I think someone sabotaged these costumes, Barb," Maggie stated plainly, after ripping off her wig and headdress so that she could speak more freely. "Just like they got rid of the scripts and destroyed my backdrop. Someone here is determined to prevent your show from going on."

"And who might that be?" Barb asked.

"I don't know yet," Maggie answered, though she fired an accusatory stare around the entire ring of suspicious cast members. "But I intend to find out exactly who is behind each of these incidents. Unless," she eyed them all again, "one of you would like to save me the trouble and confess?"

The hall dropped into an uncomfortable silence in which everyone glared at everyone else, all asking each other the silent question; "Was it you?"

A little old woman, dressed up as Benvolio because there were too few males for all the male roles, raised a bony finger, her deep sunken, pale blue eyes unblinking.

"Yes, Pam, dear, do you have something you'd like to tell us?" Maggie inquired politely.

Pam winced as she pulled the stick-on mustache from her rather furry top lip. It reddened instantly and her eyes watered, but the audience afforded her no time. Everyone wanted an answer.

"Few of you know," Pam continued in a wavering voice, "but I grew up in Blooming Hill. So I was around when Buttercup Villa was actually a holiday resort."

"Get to the point, Pam," Barb urged her. "We're not here for one of your boring history lessons."

Pam nodded rapidly and swallowed. She looked petrified. "When I was a little girl, the town would put on community plays every year for the public to enjoy. But decades ago, it all stopped."

"And why's that?" Barb asked, after polishing her red fingernails on the front of Benedict's jacket.

"Because the town ghost told us to," came Pam's shivery response.

There was an appropriate gasp from everyone assembled, followed by muttered denials or approvals.

"There's no such thing as ghosts," Sylvia replied in an almost bored tone.

"That's what we all said," Pam continued, her face gaunt and her eyes haunted. "Until the scripts all caught fire one afternoon. We wrote it off as an accident, but a few days later our costumes were shredded, much like these are. The ghost was not happy about being scoffed at."

"Well, perhaps someone didn't want the play to go on then either," Barb commented with a nervous laugh that echoed shrilly around the hall.

"That's what my parents thought. But then one of the lead characters nearly died on stage and we realized the ghost was quite serious."

An eerie silence encroached on them. Eyes flicked over shoulders and around the dimly hit hall with tall ceilings and long, blood-red dusty curtains. Billy was still trying to cover up all the red paint on the backdrop. Red paint which still looked remarkably like blood.

"Did anything happen to the backdrop?" Maggie asked Pam. "In the days of the ghost?"

Pam frowned, her thick eyebrows crossing in the middle. "Not that I can remember."

"Then the ghost is acting out of character," Maggie mumbled more to herself. "Adding to his crimes."

"You don't believe a word of this hogwash, do you, Magdalene?" Barb scoffed.

Pam turned to Barb and shook her head. "I wouldn't make fun of the ghost, Barbara," Pam whispered to her. "The lead character that nearly died was acting the role of Juliet."

Barb did not take this well. Her eyes rolled back in her head from the shock, and she reeled over and fainted, her head thudding loudly against the wooden floorboards. Since no one else had entered the space or laid a finger on Barb, rumors immediately emerged the invisible yet sinister Buttercup Villa ghost had attacked her.

Maggie groaned as the entire cast gasped in fear before making a break for the exit. She watched as some residents, bordering on ninety, sprinted as though walking sticks and hip replacements were a thing of the past.

Reginald came hobbling past her, and Maggie swore he wore the unmistakable signs of a suppressed grin.

"I suppose you're fairly pleased about all this," Maggie directed at him.

He spun around, the grin dropping off his face as his expression turned to one of sour shock.

"What's that supposed to mean?" Reginald demanded, his jaw shaking with every word.

"This morning you complained about your man stockings, and by this afternoon they've been completely destroyed. How convenient."

"In case you hadn't noticed," Reginald pointed out, his finger waving in her face, "everyone's costumes were destroyed."

"I had noticed. And I thought that's exactly what I would do if I didn't want anyone to suspect me," Maggie countered, her rosebud mouth twitching up into a smug smile.

"How dare you! You're out of your mind this time, Magdalene," Reginald informed her with an angry shake of his fist. "You're the only one in the world who could accuse her friends of doing something so terrible."

Maggie frowned at the accusation. She considered them all her friends. But they were still new friendships, and in her many years of experience, Maggie felt it took a long time before people unintentionally revealed their true character to patient onlookers.

"Thanks for getting us out of these costumes, Reg," another elderly man whispered as he walked by. He slapped Reginald on the back as he passed by.

Maggie raised an eyebrow. Reginald's bottom jaw wagged open and closed, and his eyes glared at her from under bristly eyebrows, while he turned the color of a ripe cherry.

"It wasn't me!" Reginald exploded. "Whatever people may conclude. Don't you think if I'd been planning to destroy all the costumes, I would've had enough sense to keep my mouth shut about how much I hated them so that I wouldn't be the first person everyone suspected!"

Sarah hurried over to see what the commotion was about, her crocks squeaking on the floorboards as usual and her face brimming with concern.

"Thank goodness, someone with a little sense," Reginald gestured towards Sarah. "Tell this woman where I was after the morning rehearsal."

Sarah's face momentarily blanked under the pressure of Reginald's demand. He rolled his eyes and tapped his elbow.

"Oh, of course. I took Reginald to his physical therapy appointment in town today. They've been working his elbow since the surgery."

"And when did we leave?"

"We left straight after the morning rehearsal," Sarah answered.

Maggie recalled Barb instructing the costumes be removed from the hall to the side room so that the red paint that had spread everywhere would not contaminate them. The costumes had still been intact.

"And when did you return?"

"We ran a little late because Reginald insisted we go out for a cup of coffee so he could thank me for taking him," Sarah explained. "So, we arrived back just as Barb instructed everyone to find their costumes."

"How perfectly timed," Maggie observed.

"So," Reginald shook his finger again, "it's completely and utterly impossible for me to be in two places at once. I believe I have. Now what do they call it?..." he trailed off and scratched at his grey stubble.

"An excuse?" Sarah offered, ever trying to be helpful.

"No, silly woman," Reginald grumbled. "A... they have to have them all the time in the cop shows. Someone who proves you didn't do the crime!"

Maggie knew exactly the word he was looking for, but she refused to give it to him. Reginald had everything a little too carefully worked out.

"Ooh," Sarah snapped her fingers excitedly, "an alibi!"

"Yes," Reginald clapped his hands. "I have an alibi. So, I would prefer it, Magdalene Belle, if you moved your investigation elsewhere. Perhaps you could try find the ghost of Buttercup Villa and talk to him."

"So, you believe the story is real?"

"Why wouldn't I?" Reginald snapped. "Now that I'm free to go, I'll make my way home. Thank you very much."

He paused and turned back to Maggie, wearing a sheepish smile.

"I don't suppose we're still on for tea and apple pie later?" Reginald asked hopefully.

Maggie bit her tongue, refusing to let the long list of clever retorts escape her lips. She was more determined than ever to get to the bottom of the mysterious accidents that kept befalling Barb's play, and so she needed her friends to still be willing to talk to her. Thankfully, she was a wonderful baker and most of the residents at Buttercup Villa could not bear to stay away for too long.

"Yes, Reggie, I'll see you later then."

"And you'd better remember your manners," Sarah scolded him ever so gently. "Maggie's only trying to help, you know."

"Then maybe she should stick to baking," Reginald grumbled as he hobbled away.

"Insufferable man," Sarah stomped a crock. "I do like him, but he can be so ghastly to people."

"He's in pain most of the time," Maggie observed. "And acute pain makes a person rather short tempered, I'm afraid. I can imagine forcing his tired and sore legs into tight stockings was torture."

"Gosh, you always see the reason behind why people are the way they are," Sarah admired.

"All it takes is a little quiet observation, dear," Maggie said with a smile.

"Shall we have some tea before the others arrive?" Sarah suggested.

"Perhaps you should first organize a stretcher and a set of extra hands to help you move, Barb. She's still passed out on the floor over there," Maggie reminded her.

Sarah slapped a hand to her mouth in shock and her eyes traversed the floorboards until she located the limp figure of Barb. Her purple hair flopped on the ground and her face still contorted with horror.

Chapter 7
The Phantom of the Opera

Maggie knocked tentatively on Barb's front door. It was eleven in the morning and Barb had not arrived at the scheduled morning rehearsal. Most people had skipped the practice anyway, since rumors of the ghost striking again had spread around the villa. Maggie worried that the play had all become too much for Barb and so she had taken it upon herself to check whether their slave-driving director was still alive.

There was no answer, but Maggie could hear haunting organ music blasting on the other side of the door. She tried the handle and discovered it was unlocked, so Maggie did what they expected any nosy neighbor to do in Buttercup Villa. She let herself inside.

Barb's place was cloaked in darkness, despite the sun shining brightly outside. Heavy purple drapes acted as a guard to any cheerful light which hoped to enter. Barb's kitchen table was littered with empty bottles and several pizza boxes, testament to her still being alive. The place looked as though they had not cleaned it in weeks, and a pile of slashed envelopes lay on a corner of the counter.

Maggie gulped. Her fingers were itching to tidy up, but she was not there for that.

"Barb?" she attempted to call, but some atrocious singing to *The Phantom of the Opera* drowned out her voice. Opera was not Barb's strong suit.

Maggie plunged further into the ominous abode of Barb Bristle. She followed the sound of music to Barb's bedroom door and was just about to knock when Barb herself flew out of the depths of her room singing at full volume and sloshing red wine on the carpet. She was dressed in a long, black cloak that fastened at her throat. An old-fashioned and corseted dress peeped out from underneath her cloak. The smudged make-up and dark rings under her eyes suggested she had not slept for a while.

Barb screeched in fright at the unexpected intruder and retreated into her room like a vampire shielding herself from the burn of sunlight. The stench of wine radiated from Barb and her reactions were ridiculously delayed as she swayed away from Maggie.

"It's only me, Barb," Maggie called after the strange woman. "I just came to see if you were alright."

Barb cut the music and minutes later she stepped out looking rather embarrassed. The cloak had disappeared under a thick dressing gown, which made Barb look almost normal again.

"I didn't mean to interrupt your solo performance," Maggie assured her. "One of my favorite musicals, by the way."

"What do you want, Ms. Belle?" Barb demanded, the dark make-up making her look harsh and cruel.

"You didn't show at rehearsal this morning," Maggie informed her. "I was worried."

"What are you talking about?" Barb snapped while forcing her way past Maggie and into the filth of her kitchen. "It's eleven at night."

"It's eleven in the morning," Maggie corrected her.

Barb flicked a dubious eyebrow up, forcing Maggie to wrench open a curtain and scald Barb with morning sunshine.

"Close it!" Barb hissed, her arms shielding her face.

"What's going on with you, Barb?" Maggie asked gently. "This is not you. You used to prune roses in your front garden every morning."

"You've only been here a few months so you don't know the real me," Barb fired back.

Maggie sighed, the heavy basket on her arm weighing her down.

"When last have you eaten a decent meal?"

Barb folded her arms across her chest and studied her big toe poking out of its sock.

"I'll take that as a long time. Why don't you go take a shower, and I'll sort out your kitchen," Maggie insisted rather than suggested.

"I don't need to shower, and I don't need you fussing over me. I'm a grown woman!"

"I know you are," Maggie soothed, while laying a hand on Barb's back and shoving her gently towards the bathroom. "Nice hot shower, and don't forget to wash your hair. You've got what looks like a slice of pepperoni stuck in it."

Barb grumbled the entire way into the bathroom, but once the door was shut, and Maggie could hear running water, she set about fixing a clean space to work in the kitchen.

Maggie hummed gently as popped two homemade steak pies onto a tray and set them in the oven. Maggie always felt that when someone was feeling glum, a piece of buttery, flakey homemade pastry went a long way in cheering them up.

With the pies heating through and crisping up in the oven, Maggie set about peeling some potatoes and chopping them into chunky strips. Once they were frying away, Maggie began a fresh garden salad. Baby tomatoes Billy had brought her from his home garden. Feta cheese, lettuce, cucumber, and olives were all slapped into a bowl and drizzled generously with olive oil and balsamic vinegar.

By the time a cleaner and fresher version of Barb stepped out of her room wearing a plain t-shirt and a pair of track pants, Maggie thought the overly dramatic woman looked almost normal. Barb followed her nose to the kitchen table, which she stared down at in shock.

"So, this is what the wood looked like under all that junk," Barb joked.

Maggie had located two placemats, some clean cutlery, and had even snatched a rose from the courtyard garden for the center of the table.

"Sit," Maggie ordered, before Barb could start complaining again.

Barb obeyed and watched as Maggie dished up a heap of salad, followed by some salty potatoes, and finally a crisp short crust pastry pie, which oozed thick steak gravy and smelled of mouthwatering deliciousness.

"What's all this?" Barb asked half timidly, her voice for the stage neatly packed away.

"I thought with all the pressure you're under, you're likely not finding time to cook properly," Maggie explained. "So, a decent meal is certainly in order. Juice?"

"I'd prefer the fermented grape kind," Barb joked weakly.

She received lemonade instead.

"Why are you doing all this?" Barb asked, fixing an intense stare on Maggie.

"Sometimes we all just need someone to look out for us."

"But I've been downright ghastly to you," Barb admitted ashamedly. "Accusing you of burning my scripts and ruining the backdrop you spent hours painting yourself. You must think I'm half mad. Although, in my defense, how was I supposed to know we had our very own theatre phantom causing all this havoc?"

"There's no ghost, Barb," Maggie stated simply. "Someone is using that tale as a cover to ruin your play."

"You really think so?"

"I do," Maggie said before taking a bite of her delicious pie. "Eat up before it gets cold."

"But who would do such a thing?"

"I'm not sure yet. Everyone is both suspicious and innocent I'm afraid. It makes investigating a little hard."

Barb mulled this over while she took a long drink from her lemonade. "I can't believe I didn't sleep last night."

"You must be exhausted."

"After the whole ghost thing yesterday, I just couldn't take it anymore. I was standing there watching everyone freak out about a ghost, and I thought, what if it's all true? What if we never get to perform the play? What if I really end up getting hurt, as the previous Juliet was? Is this my end? A cruel death on stage? Life taken away too soon… I can just see the headlines."

"What if we catch whoever is behind this?" Maggie interrupted with a smile and a twinkle in her eye.

Barb snorted. She quietly pondered her predicament while chewing on another forkful of pie.

"I appreciate your taking an interest in me and coming in here and pulling me out of wherever hole I was stuck inside, but I'm not about to play Watson to your Sherlock," Barb replied with an air of mockery. "I simply have no time for that."

It mildly hurt Maggie. With a bit of food in her and a sobering bout in the shower, Barb had emerged her old, aloof self who felt empowered by pushing Maggie down.

"No," Barb ran her long nails through her tangled, wet curls, "the show will go on. I was ridiculous for believing anyone, or anything, could stop me from producing the best play this town has ever seen."

"I wouldn't expect any less," Maggie replied stiffly while she scraped the scraps from Barb's plate into her own. "I have one more question, though."

"You can't have Juliet back, just because you were nice to me," Barb snapped rather tartly.

She was definitely rekindling her old fire again, and Maggie was feeling progressively more uncomfortable.

"Why is this play so important to you?"

Barb squinted at her as if trying to work out what Maggie's angle was. They sat in silence while Barb considered whether to tell Maggie what was really on her mind. She opened her mouth and looked as though she was about to open up, when an Abba tune chortled from the bedroom as a monotone ringtone.

"My cellphone," Barb said with excusing herself. "Probably someone important."

She stood up and disappeared into her bedroom, the door slamming behind her. Maggie sighed and started packing her basket with the things she had brought over. She thought it might take a few more meals, but eventually, with time, she would soften Barb's tough heart enough for it to be opened up.

The problem was that Maggie did not have the time. Her eyes scanned Barb's crowded countertop for a clue of any kind. Something that would give her insight into what was driving Barb mad about the production. She remembered the torn envelopes and quickly located them again. Technically, she was not doing anything illegal if the envelopes were already opened.

The bold, red print across the front of several envelopes alerted her to the possibility that something was very wrong.

Maggie checked that Barb's bedroom door was still closed, before slipping a finger into the envelope and pulling out the contents.

"Oh my," Maggie whispered to herself as she scanned the notice.

She opened the next two letters and found similar words of threat. All the pieces flew together. The empty fridge, the filthy home, and the takeout and cheap liquor bottles. Barb was desperately broke. There was no money to pay the rent, let alone a cleaner, or purchase the villa's healthy cooked meals.

Maggie's heart throbbed against her chest as she realized Barb had been facing the prospect of bankruptcy and homelessness alone. She had not confided in any of them. Instead, she had come up with some twisted solution where she worked herself to death, putting on a performance to bring money in for tyrant Michelle. Perhaps the play was not just for publicity, but a way for Barb to pay off the debt she owed Michelle.

Whatever the reason, Barb only had a couple of weeks to settle everything before Michelle promised to remove the old woman from her lodgings. She wondered what she would do if they caught her in a situation like Barb's. Her mind strayed to her loving daughter, who would likely come up with a plan to pay the outstanding debt. Barb had never mentioned family or friends who could be there for her. And Maggie realized that Barb received no visitors either.

Maggie sighed as she slipped the letters back to their original spot, her mind churning as it tried to come up with a way to help Barb. Barb's voice had faded from inside her room, so Maggie knocked gently on the door. It creaked open, so she poked her head inside to check if Barb was okay.

Barb was lying face down on her bed, a gentle snore escaping in between breaths. Maggie carefully closed the door behind her, content to let Barb get some rest while she used the time to come up with a plan.

Chapter 8
Tea Party and
Garden Confession

"Right, now I've assembled you all here because there's something important that we need to discuss," Maggie began, after they had settled everyone down with a cup of coffee and an almond croissant from the bakery.

"I agree," Benedict interrupted. "Barb cannot be allowed to continue as Juliet."

There was an approving cheer from the small group, but Benedict, having glimpsed Maggie's stern eye, quietly lowered himself back into his seat and disappeared behind a buttery croissant.

"Now I know that we have all struggled under the iron fist of Barb Bristle," Maggie began again. "And the long hours of rehearsal and –"

"It's not that we don't enjoy a bit of Shakespeare," Reggie interrupted. "I'm quite enamored by the prospect of taking on a bit of acting in my old age. The only problem is Barb. She's too bossy. Won't listen to reason."

"Exactly," Sylvia pushed her way into the conversation. "Barb has always believed herself better than the rest of us, but it's as though the play has given her an opportunity to lord her superiority over us without restraint."

"Now, if you'll just give me a minute," Maggie attempted again, "I really do think you'll find that what I have to tell you about Barb explains a lot of things."

"And you, of all people, Maggie," Benedict spoke up again. "The way Barbara has treated you, has been absolutely atrocious. You're no Nurse. You were born to be a Juliet."

"That's really not important, right now, Ben," Maggie said earnestly, as she tried to get back on track.

"You know, I think we should all stand together and approach Barb as a united front," Reginald suggested, his old war instincts kicking in.

"What do you mean?" Sylvia asked, intrigued. "Like with clubs and burning torches?"

"No, we're not a group of savage villagers out for blood. I simply meant we could explain that we are perfectly happy to perform the play for the public, but on one condition," Reginald continued with a twinkle in his old cataracted eye.

"And what would that be?" Benedict asked, taking the bait.

"That she can organize from behind the scenes but will no longer be in charge of us. We will run the play for ourselves, and choose our own costumes," Reginald stated with a thump of his walking stick on the floorboards.

Sylvia and Benedict shared a second long look before they both erupted into laughter.

"You honestly believe," Sylvia said in between snorts, "that drama queen Barb will willingly walk away from a production that has her name printed on the posters decorating every wall in town?"

"You're out of your mind with this idea, Reggie, old chap. Barb wouldn't dream of handing the play over to us amateurs," Benedict disagreed. "Besides, we do sort of need her. We just have to bring in the reins a little."

"Then perhaps Barb could be persuaded in another way," Reggie reasoned.

"I don't care what Barb does or doesn't do. My only concern is that I'm not kissing her," Benedict stated firmly, his arms folding defensively across his chest. "I refuse."

"Oh, but you're happy to kiss Maggie, are you?" Reggie insinuated with an exaggerated wink.

Benedict looked at Maggie with a coy smile, which provided an unspoken answer to Reginald's question.

"Well, you might be confident," Sylvia teased, "but I'm not so sure Maggie's entirely happy with having your flirty lips lock on hers."

Maggie slumped down into her chair and sank her teeth into a flakey croissant. She hoped a taste of sugary goodness would help lighten the blow of her failed attempt to communicate with her friends. As she looked from face to face, Maggie tried not to feel the critical burn of disproval in her heart, and to tried instead to focus on how good they could be. It was hard to hide the disappointment written on every wrinkle of her sad face.

"Don't be too hard on yourself," Sarah whispered next to her.

Maggie had not noticed that the young, auburn-haired nurse had pulled up a chair next to her.

"What are you doing here?"

"I came to bring everyone their morning meds," Sarah explained. "I saw what happened, and I can tell by the look on your face that you're not impressed. Did you figure out why Barb's being an extra mean Barb?"

Maggie nodded. Benedict and Reginald were busy reenacting the sword fight scene between Romeo and Paris. Reginald was swinging one of his walking sticks wildly, narrowly missing the overhanging lampshade.

"Barb's in trouble," Maggie explained. "I think she's behind on her rent and that's why she's so hellbent on making this play work. The money may help her pay off her debt."

"Surely we can come together and help her out?" Sarah said while dabbing her handkerchief at her eyes. She had one of the softest hearts Maggie had ever encountered.

"I'm working on it. I hoped that by talking to the group, we could come up with a plan to help Barb, but they're all a little preoccupied with their own concerns about the play."

"Why don't you just speak up," Sarah urged her. Maggie watched as the nurse stood up and cleared her throat until she had everyone's attention. "Sorry to interrupt your little rehearsal, but Maggie has something important she needs to tell you about Barb."

All eyes turned to Maggie, and they waited, briefly quiet and expectant.

Maggie took a deep breath. "I think Barb is in real trouble."

"Of course she is," Sylvia continued, "it was said as much at the rehearsal yesterday. Pam has lived in this town her whole life. If she says there's a ghost that haunts the theatre, then I believe her and Barb had better watch her step."

With that the conversation escalated rather excitedly about the so-called phantom that was going to off Barb if she did not step down as Juliet.

Maggie found she could no longer endure the vapid complaints and critical jests. She set her coffee mug on the table and stormed out of her little cottage as fast as her arthritic hips and knees would allow her to go. Really, it was a rather slow amble instead. Maggie did not glance back, knowing that her self-involved group of so-called friends did not even notice her absence.

"Maggie," a voice called, and a hand touched her elbow. "What's going on?"

Benedict gazed at her out of striking blue eyes that had not dulled with age. He had noticed.

Maggie shook her arm out of his. "Now you want to listen?"

"What do you mean by that?" Benedict asked, withdrawing his arm with a hurt expression.

"I've been trying to tell the group something important for the last thirty minutes, but no one was interested. Including you."

"I'm always interested in what you have to say," he offered gently. "I care deeply about you…" he paused, his eyes finding his shoes instead of her gaze. "I know you think I've probably said that to a ton of women in my life."

"I bet you have," Maggie retorted, unsure of where Benedict was going with his usual flirtatious charm.

"But I really mean it. I care about you, Maggie, and I want to be around you all the time," Benedict said, making a reach for her hand again. "I didn't think that I'd find anyone this late in my life, but here we are."

"Benedict, what are you saying?" Maggie stammered, panic rising in her chest.

"I think I really want you to be my Juliet. That's why I've been going to these lengths to get you back in your role. I love spending time with you."

Maggie's jaw dropped, and she found words danced away from her tongue before she found the strength to say them out loud.

"Oh, come on, old girl," Benedict seized both her shaking hands, "please tell me you feel the same way?"

Maggie swallowed, her throat instantly dry and her palms sweating inside Benedict's. She had been a widow for a good ten years and had not had a man hold her hands since then.

"I'm afraid you've taken me quite by surprise, Ben, and I don't think I can provide you with the answer you want," Maggie admitted in a whisper.

She became conscious of the inquisitive pale faces looming at the windowpanes of her cottage, looking out hoping to see if Benedict was having any luck. He must have told Sylvia and Reginald about his feelings long before he confessed them to Maggie. This only made her feel even more excluded from their little group.

"They tried to warn me. They said a woman of your caliber would never be interested in someone like me," Benedict stated numbly, his hands falling away from hers.

"Benedict, listen to yourself. You don't even know what kind of woman I am," Maggie pointed out. "And I don't really know much about you. We were strangers a couple of months ago."

"I know you care about other people, and you always try to help them. That's one thing I like about you. You're unselfish, unlike me. I've spent the last seven decades thinking entirely about myself. But meeting you has made me want to change."

"I appreciate that you think you admire me for that, but if that was really true, then surely you would listen to me when I try to tell you about someone I think we need to help?"

Benedict's brow creased with frown lines and he shook his head. "What are you talking about?"

"Exactly my point," Maggie said. "You like the idea of me, Benedict. Because I'm new in town and the concept of new excites you. But you do not know how to commit to me or anyone else. You never stop and take the time to listen."

Benedict dropped his head, his eyes avoiding hers. "I will not give up," he muttered, to her surprise.

Maggie did not know what to say and so she let him stride past her in an air of dejection and out of the garden. She expected him to slam her white picket gate, but then she remembered Benedict was always a gentleman at heart. Even when his heart was in pieces, his manners remained perfectly intact.

Maggie sighed deeply and looked up at her cottage. Eager faces spotted hers and then disappeared behind the drapes again.

"I think it's time for everyone to go home," she announced loudly.

She waited patiently as Sylvia, Reginald, and Pam all hurried out of her cottage and down the walkway. Sarah followed shortly after.

"I'll check in on you later. I've got a patient I have to see now," Sarah informed her. She smiled warmly and squeezed Maggie's arm. "All this nonsense will sort itself out. Don't think too deeply about all this."

"I'll try," Maggie lied.

With her cottage vacated, Maggie cleared up the coffee mugs and croissant-flaked plates. She washed the dishes, wiped down all the surfaces, and plumped the couch cushions again before returning to her armchair with a cup of tea and a piece of knitting she had been struggling with for the last two weeks.

As she knitted row after row, the soft click of steel needles against each other soothing her anxious nerves, Maggie disappeared into a deep cloud of thought. She replayed all the incidents in order of their occurrence. It had all begun with Robert setting off the sprinklers so they could all have a break from rehearsals. But Robert had easily confessed. Next, there had been the scripts which she had thought Sylvia had rigged to catch fire, but Sylvia had Sarah as an alibi, since they had both been stitching costumes.

Then there was the backdrop, dripping with angry red paint. Maggie could not shake the feeling that they had directed the backdrop attack her way. Billy had been working tirelessly to fix up a lot of the mess, especially since

Maggie could not find the will to pick up her brush again, after her work had been so callously destroyed the first time.

Finally, the costumes had been savaged. Maggie had assumed Reginald was the culprit since he had seemed to have the most issues with the appearance of the costumes, but he had been at a doctor's appointment.

"Nothing makes sense," Maggie said, almost as though she was scolding herself for missing the obvious.

She clicked her tongue when she realized she had dropped a stich several rows before and was staring at a gaping hole in her carefully worked out pattern. She dropped her knitting to her knee and looked at her wristwatch. A full ten minutes before their afternoon rehearsal was due to start.

Chapter 9
The Gift Horse
Comes Bearing Wine

Maggie arrived five minutes late. It was not in her nature to be late, but she did not want to do the friendly mill around chatting while waiting for Barb to start. To her surprise, all the actors were still sitting around, wearing various patched up items of clothing and stitched up stockings, all except Reginald, whose stockings were beyond repair. He wore a pair of slacks.

Sarah hurried in after Maggie, carrying a piece of scrunched up paper in her hand. She mounted the stage with the help of Benedict and cleared her throat so that she could have everyone's attention.

"Sorry ladies and gentlemen, but I have a note from Barb," she informed them. "It reads: 'I cannot make rehearsals this evening as I am unwell. Since we are so close to our public performance, this forces me to step down as Juliet. I appoint Maggie to her original role. Please continue rehearsals without me. You need all the practice you can get as we're already sold out and the show must go on, with or without me, though I suspect you all prefer the latter.'"

There was a loud cheer from the cast of actors as everyone spun round, expecting to find a happy Maggie, whereas, to their surprise, they found no Maggie at all.

Maggie knocked on the familiar door again, hoping her presence would be more welcome than it was the night before.

"Come in," Barb's voice groaned from deep inside her cottage.

Maggie obeyed and quickly hurried inside, before anyone realized she had left the hall. The living room was swathed in darkness again and the pungent air smelled sour, a sure sign that Barb really was sick.

"Who is it?" Barb called again in a scratchy voice.

"It's me," Maggie announced, letting herself into Barb's bedroom. "I heard you were sick, and I came to see if it was really so."

Barb was lying in bed, covered with a duvet and a blanket. She looked pale and cold, breaking out in a shiver now and then, while a film of sweat spread across her clammy forehead. Her eyes were sunken deep, and her hair was damp and clung to the skin around her face.

"What do you think?"

"I'd say you look downright awful," Maggie observed with a twitch of a smile. "What did Sarah diagnose?"

"She's given me some meds and something to hydrate my system. My stomach just exploded. I actually told Sarah I believed it was your fault."

"My fault?" Maggie repeated in disbelief.

"Your pie. I thought you had tried to poison me so that you could get your hands back on the role of Juliet. But Sarah scolded me for that one. She claimed you were helping me out of the goodness of your heart and that since you ate one pie yourself, it was unlikely you could have been responsible for my sudden decline in health."

"Thank goodness you listened to Sarah. Did she make you write the note?" Maggie asked, still slightly aghast that Barb had thought she would cause her harm.

"Yes," Barb chuckled breathlessly.

"I really didn't poison you, Barb," Maggie stated firmly. "Though there are others who wanted you gone as Juliet. Did anyone else bring you something to eat?"

Barb shook her head. "Sarah reasoned it's all the alcohol and takeout, paired with an immense amount of stress that likely broke my system. I'll be alright in a day or two once my stomach has settled a bit. Would you mind fetching me something to drink? Sarah put a rehydration concoction in the fridge. She said she would check me into the hospital if I didn't drink it all."

Maggie smiled and left the room. Something did not feel right about Barb's sudden illness. She opened the fridge and poured Barb a glass of some potent smelling orange liquid. Before returning to the bedroom, Maggie glanced around for anything else that had changed from the night before.

The kitchen was certainly tidier, but she suspected that Sarah had had something to do with that. There was a wine glass in the sink, stained red at the bottom. Barb had certainly been drinking the cheap stuff the night before, but there was an empty expensive wine bottle in the bin.

"If Barb was so broke, how would she have been able to afford expensive wine?" Maggie muttered to herself.

She slipped on her reading glasses and pulled out the cork, studying the rim of the green wine bottle. Tiny specks of white powder dusted the edge of one side. Maggie sniffed at it, but her old nose could distinguish nothing other than the smell of sour wine.

Barb croaked something about needing liquid, so Maggie jumped up and carried the juice to her.

"Sip it slowly," Maggie ordered. "I have an odd question for you. Did anyone drop off a bottle of wine last night?"

Barb scowled at her. "Going through my trash, are we?"

"Just answer the question," Maggie ordered gently.

"There was a bottle on my doorstep at lunch time. It came with a card that said, 'Sorry.' I assumed someone was apologizing for all the hell I've been through with the play, so I drank up."

"Did you notice or taste anything unusual about it?"

Barb cocked an eyebrow. "Not that I can recall. It had been opened, though. The cork was just shoved back in."

"And what happened after you drank it?"

"What's with all the questions?" Barb complained. "I'm sick and weak, and you're interrogating me endlessly."

"I think someone slipped something into your drink. When did you start feeling sick?"

"After lunch…" Barb's voice trailed off. "My gosh, I think you're right. I couldn't keep out of the bathroom after I drank the wine."

"It's certainly no coincidence that you suddenly fell sick before one of our big rehearsals. Somebody did not want you there today. I think the note saying 'sorry' was an apology for what was about to happen to you."

Barb paled drastically and her jaw dropped open, revealing a set of pearly white false teeth.

"Do you think…" her lip quivered, "that the phantom really is out to get me? What if this was…" she glanced around, her eyes wide with terror, "a warning shot?"

"Barb, I don't think there really is a phantom, or a ghost, or anything supernatural about what's going on here, because why would a ghost go to all the trouble to put laxatives in a rather expensive bottle of wine and render you partly inactive?"

Barb frowned again. "You have a point there," she said with an embarrassed chuckle. "Alright, so someone's out to give me the runs. I suppose that's better than death. What do we do now?"

"I'm still working on that," Maggie replied, her finger tapping on her chin while she thought.

"I still don't get why you're helping me," Barb mumbled. "No one else cares. Except Sarah, but she's paid to as a nurse here, so it doesn't count."

"Barb, I need to come clean about something. I know about your debt," Maggie admitted.

Barb lurched bolt upright. "How could you possibly…" she trailed off and realization spread through her features. "You found Michelle's threatening letters. So, you're not such a genius after all. Just a snooper."

"It was wrong of me to snoop, I know, but I knew something was going on and you were refusing to tell me," Maggie explained in a nervous ramble of words.

"That's the last time I open my door to you," Barb snorted, though there was more amusement than anger on her face.

"At least I didn't lace your wine with something nasty," Maggie teased.

Barb managed a weak chuckle before her eyes snapped open and she rapidly wormed her way out of bed, pushing past Maggie.

"Excuse me," she groaned before slamming the bathroom door shut.

"I'll let myself out then," Maggie yelled after her. "I'm late for a rehearsal, after all."

Chapter 10
Whiskey Cures
a Broken Heart

It had been a long afternoon of rehearsing. Things had been beyond awkward on stage, and the lines delivered with about as much enthusiasm as if they had come from a hard-boiled egg. Benedict, having finally gotten Maggie back as his beloved Juliet, could barely look her in the eye after her candid rejection, let alone be enticed to kiss her.

It did not help matters that Michelle was stalking around like a vulture circling prey, waiting to leap on them if they said an incorrect line or duffed up a cue. By the time they were finished, everyone was exhausted, and they drifted off stage completely depleted.

"We just can't do it without Barb's zeal and flare fueling us on," Pam announced to the group.

She was promptly stared down into silence, but Maggie got the feeling that Pam was not the only one missing Barb's guidance from the front lines. The group had arranged a second rehearsal for the following day, hoping everyone's spirits would be lifted and things would run better.

Maggie felt depressed as she made her way home that evening. To cheer herself up, she took an extra-long soak in a hot tub of water, with a few drops of lavender essential oil to calm her nerves and ease the pain of her old joints. She then dressed, wrapped herself in a warm gown and hobbled off to the kitchen, her skin still rosy-pink from the glorious heat of the bathroom.

She had just settled into her armchair with a hefty ham sandwich and a small whiskey when there was an urgent knock on the door. Maggie felt her stomach churn. She was not quite ready to face her group of so-called friends after the uneasiness of that afternoon. She bit her lip in panic at the thought of Benedict coming to tell her off for rejecting him.

"It's only me, Sarah!" came a call through the wood.

"Come in," Maggie gushed with relief.

She felt Sarah was the one person she could still trust, apart from her ever loyal Billy.

"I thought you were supposed to be on your blind date tonight?" Maggie shouted over her shoulder while shuffling to the kitchen to pull out a teacup.

"It's already over," came the glum reply that forced Maggie to turn around and give her friend a good look over.

Sarah was wearing a hideous red polka dot dress. Her hair had been curled, though it looked damp and sticky, and it hung limply around her distraught face. She had red lipstick smudged halfway across her face and mascara stains down both cheeks. As she stepped in and closed the door behind her, Maggie could hear the unmistakable squelch of something liquid moving around the inside of her shoes.

"What on earth happened to you, dear?" Maggie asked in astonishment. She was so focused on Sarah, she did not notice she had overfilled the teapot and water was flowing onto the floor.

"It's a long story. I don't feel like going home looking like this when I'm still supposed to be on my date for another two hours. Would you mind if I -"

"Of course not, dear. There are clean towels in the cupboard, and I'll find you something comfortable to slip into."

As a miserable Sarah trudged past, Maggie got a distinct whiff of champagne mixed with perfume, cigarette smoke and a man's cologne. Sarah's stockings were laddered and ripped and clumped around her ankles, and even one of her dress straps was torn.

"You look a right mess, Sarah," Maggie stated in shock.

Sarah hopped into the shower and re-emerged twenty minutes later with her hair in a towel and her body smelling of lavender shower gel. Maggie's pink tracksuit pants and matching hoodie were a little too small for Sarah, and so her ankles and wrists poked out, but she looked far more relaxed.

"Sit," Maggie ordered. "Hungry?"

"Starved."

"I'll make you a ham sandwich and you get talking."

"Oh, Mags," Sarah exploded, her arms waving wildly and her eyes wide with distress, "it was an utter failure. An absolute disaster of note! Why did I ever believe for a moment that I could go on a date and find happiness? It's never worked for me in the past."

Maggie handed Sarah a double shot of whiskey, which Sarah kicked back in one go.

"Another."

"Alright then," Maggie mumbled as she made her way back to the bottle. So much for Sarah never drinking.

"At first, everything was okay. He was the perfect gentleman. He picked me up on time, led me into the restaurant on his arm, and paraded me around like I was the most beautiful woman there."

"So, what went wrong?"

"He didn't like the restaurant. So, we went over to the pub. More his style, he said. He sat us in a quiet booth near the bar and ordered a heavy round of drinks."

"Oh dear."

"And then another round," Sarah gestured widely. "I was still sipping my first, and he kept piling them up while he slugged through each one in record speed."

"Well, it was Benedict's choice of a friend," Maggie pointed out with a bitter dig at her flirty neighbor. "That should've been warning enough that the evening would go badly."

"Then Max ordered a bottle of champagne. But he was so drunk at this point that he ended up spraying the bottle all over me. Of course, he thought this was the most hilarious thing to happen all evening, and he got the entire bar cheering along with him."

"How awful," Maggie gasped fittingly, while filling Sarah's glass for the third time.

"Then he got really flirty," Sarah whispered. "He slunk in close next to me and breathed boozy air in my face. I honestly tried to make conversation, but he looked as though he was going to pass out, so I sort of shook him by his jacket lapels."

Sarah turned bright red and sank into her armchair while hiding behind a frilly cushion with roses embroidered on the front. A tuft of wet auburn hair stuck out the top.

"Don't tell me he thought you were making a move on him," Maggie guessed.

"He did!" Sarah shrieked in absolute mortification. "And he wasted no time in planting his brandy-flavored lips on mine and sucking my will to live out of me."

Maggie fought back a giggle. It was tragic that the first date Sarah had bravely embarked on since her hideous divorce had resulted in a desperate man laying his all too quickly puckered lips on hers.

"I tried to pull away, but his sleeve hooked in my hair, and then in the awful process of losing a clump of hair to his cufflink, my dress strap snapped off and I popped out half a boob."

Maggie hid her smile with a hand. She could not laugh at her friend in her moment of need.

"I quickly covered up, but it was too late," Sarah was pacing up and down Maggie's lounge, her near-empty whiskey glass dangling from one hand. "He thought I was making another move on him, so he laid a hand on my knee and moved in for another lip locker."

"Oh, Sarah, dear," Maggie sympathized as best she could.

"That's when I made a run for it. My legs were all tangled up in his, and I was half stuck to my seat from all the champagne, but I clawed my way out of the booth, losing my stockings and dignity. I lied and said I was bringing another round, and the second he was distracted by the charms of a younger..." she sniffed, tears welling up in her eyes, "and more beautiful woman, I bolted for my life."

Sarah sobbed loudly. It was not the pretty cry that actresses spent hours practicing in the mirror. It was the ugly kind that scared away spouses and small children.

"There, there," Maggie soothed, removing the glass from Sarah's hand. "We should have known any friend of Benedict's would only cause heartbreak and embarrassment."

Sarah paused mid-cry and stared at Maggie. "That's the second time you've brought up Benedict in a derogatory tone. What happened today when the two of you were chatting out in the garden?"

Maggie's smile faded. She had hoped that Sarah had forgotten about that.

"Oh, nothing," Maggie shook her head. She realized Sarah had shared a humiliating story with her and so it was only fair she reveal something of her own feelings. "Benedict believes himself in love with me, and I turned him down. Whether or not it was foolish, I do not know. How can I relinquish my heart, even a smidgen, to a man who proclaims his love to half the women in the community?"

"Exactly," Sarah proclaimed loudly and with a slight sway. She raised her glass and tapped it with a loud clang against Maggie's before missing her mouth and sloshing the remainder down her front.

"Alright, that's enough whiskey for you, dear. I'll telephone your father and explain you'll be spending the night with me. No driving, or even walking, for you, young lady."

Sarah giggled and snuck another few fingers of whiskey into her glass while it forced Maggie to make polite conversation on the phone to Cedric. He proved himself a brilliant policeman and after one minute of interrogation, he had worked out that his daughter was, in fact, drunk and sulking, and not spending the night with her blind date.

"You're the only real friend I have," Sarah admitted, her drunkenness rapidly reaching the serious stage, where wrought emotions are laid bare.

"To be honest, Sarah dear, you're the only real friend I have here, too."

"What about the others? They adore your company and decided they liked you the day you arrived here."

Maggie sighed. "I just don't know who they are. Trust is very important to me in a friendship."

Sarah sighed. "Can't trust Benedict. Or his lousy friends. You know, I thought for once, just once, I might end up meeting a nice guy. Instead, I get showered in champagne and have him grab my boob under false pretenses."

There was a loud thump on the front door. The knocker only waited a few seconds before plunging into the room.

"Benedict!" Maggie squeaked in surprise, while wrenching the front of her gown over her pink rosebud pajamas.

The tall man stared from the whiskey bottle to the empty glasses, and back to the glaring faces of the scorned women who directed all their fury his way.

"I came as soon as I heard," Benedict blurted out, his eyes on Sarah. "I did not know Max would be such an idiot. Honest, Sarah. I would never set you up with a complete drunk, you know that. Max was my most decent of friends."

"Do I?" Sarah fired, backed up by a fair amount of liquid courage. "Maggie says he's just like you!"

Maggie saw the hurt rip through his face. He clenched and unclenched his fist, and she noticed his knuckles were purple and swollen.

"I didn't quite say that. What happened to your hand?" Maggie asked.

Benedict sighed and wiped a hand down his face. "I was out with some friends when a drunk Max found me and complained about his date, which was 'all tease and no fun.' He said you'd fled. I took one look at his state, and knowing that you are an absolute gem of a lady, Sarah, I knew he had to have been at fault."

"So, you hit him?" Sarah gasped.

"I'm afraid I did bop him one on the nose after we got into a long argument. I was just so furious. He was supposed to show you a good time, Sarah. After he passed out on the pub floor, I learned his girlfriend had dumped him and left him in a terrible mess. He was not the Max I was expecting for you. The Max I knew didn't even drink, which is why I thought he'd be good for you. You have to believe I would never -"

Sarah had walked over and took Benedict by his injured hand.

"I know," Sarah said simply. "Thank you for standing up for me. I'm sorry it was such a disaster. To be honest, I thought there had to be something wrong with me for the guy to get drunk within four minutes of meeting me."

"There's nothing wrong with you, my sweet, sweet darling Sarah," Benedict assured her. "If I was twenty years younger…"

"Try forty," Maggie interrupted.

"Well, you get the point. Even then, I suppose I wouldn't wish a man like me on a heart of gold like yours."

Sarah teared up again, the loud sobs following as she buried her head into Benedict's chest. Even Maggie found a lump in her throat when she thought of what Benedict had done for Sarah. He locked blue eyes with Maggie over Sarah's shoulder, and offered her the smallest of smiles.

Maggie mouthed the words, 'Thank you,' and thought for a moment about how complex people could be. She stood by her theory that you never really knew a person until they opened up and reveal an unguarded piece of their heart to you.

"Let's get your hand cleaned up," Maggie offered. "I think our local nurse is too out of it, and we can't have Romeo all beat up before his big performance even starts."

Chapter 11
Break a Leg...
or an Ankle

Maggie stepped out from backstage wearing a deep red velvety dress, with white poofy sleeves and gold brocade down the front. Her old fingers gripped onto the lengthy, dusty curtain for strength. She could relate to the old, moth-eaten drapes that likely had not been pulled shut since the last performance decades before. She believed herself too old to be prancing around on stage.

Maggie almost felt the part of the wealthy Juliet Capulet, but the layers of material were heavy, and she moved across the stage with less speed than a tortoise in hibernation, rather than a fourteen-year-old lass in the exciting grips of love.

She watched from behind the curtain as Billy cleaned up the last of his paint. He had done a fairly good job trying to imitate Maggie's painting style and correct the patches of the red paint that had marked their mural. Mia was watching him from a few feet away, her fingers twirling a long strand of blonde hair. Mia was supposed to be helping Pam into her costume, but she was oblivious to the heaving and huffing of the old woman next to her as she squeezed into a dress two sizes too small. Pam was both Benvolio and Lady Montague and so she had to wear one costume under the other.

A whistle sounded behind her, and Maggie jumped on the spot.

"You look stunning in your dress," Benedict complimented her with a smile. "I always knew you were a Juliet at heart."

Maggie dared a sidelong look. Benedict was wearing his Romeo jacket over a pair of slacks. They had discarded the tights after the slashing incident. She had to admit that Benedict looked rather handsome, all cleaned up and neatly shaven.

"I see your mustache is gone," Maggie observed.

"Yes," Benedict rubbed his chin, "it was time for a change. I'm not the man I was back then."

"What's the difference between a mustached Benedict and an un-mustached one?"

He shrugged and winked at her. "I'm not sure yet."

"Benedict, I wanted to thank you for standing up for Sarah like that. She was in low spirits last night, but I think you cheered her up."

Benedict nodded seriously. "I would never want harm to come to Sarah. And I would never willingly choose to hurt a woman I truly cared about."

Maggie felt drawn in by the intensity of his gaze. The lack of mustache gave him a more youthful and innocent look, and she had the impression that she was looking at an entirely different person.

"What do you think about those two, then?" Maggie asked with a flick of her head in Billy and Mia's direction.

"I've noticed Mia is less of her flirty self with me," Benedict observed. "Now I see why. Billy sure has manned up since he started here. He caught Mia's eye.

"I'm rather protective of him," Maggie admitted. "I don't want to interfere, but I'd hate Billy to have a broken heart. He reciprocates her feelings, I think.

"We all experience a broken heart at some stage or another. 'Better to have loved and lost.'" Benedict nudged her with his elbow.

"Anyway, we should probably get started. I never expected everything to come together like it has. Things feel almost quite professional."

"Barb would be proud," Benedict chuckled.

"Barb is not proud," came Barb's voice.

She strode out confidently from the shadows, wearing Juliet's white and gold wedding dress. All the assembled actors gasped in shock.

"B-barb," Benedict stuttered.

"Yes, B-benedict?" Barb mocked him.

"I thought you were too unwell to play the part? We got your letter."

"Did you now?" Barb replied in an unconcerned drawl. "Well, I am vastly improved. I think all the sleep added another decade to my lifespan. I've never felt better."

"We're glad to hear it, Barb," Maggie piped up.

Barb x-rayed Maggie with an unblinking stare, an eyebrow finally spiking.

"What on earth are you dressed as Juliet for?" Barb snapped. "Put on Nurse's clothes."

"But, I thought," Maggie stumbled over her words, her cheeks reddening despite the layer of stage rouge.

"You thought wrong," Barb informed her before striding confidently away into the middle of the stage. "Attention everyone," she announced loudly to the group of startled residents. "I'm perfectly healthy and thus I'm taking control of this production once again. Hop to, we're starting from act one scene one, in five."

Everyone watched, mouths agape, as Barb marched across the wooden stage, her Elizabethan heels thudding loudly against the creaking floorboards. As Barb neared the center of the stage, her foot smashed through the floor. Seconds later, the floor beneath her seemed to cave in and gulp Barb downwards, until only her torso was sticking out.

Pam and Sylvia screamed, but even their combined effort was out-screamed by Barb's shrill shriek for help. The men leapt quickly into action. Well, as quickly as they could. Reginald took several minutes trying to hobble up the stage wing steps. A paint-streaked Billy was the first to arrive, followed by Benedict. Together, and with a lot of huffing and puffing on Benedict's side, they grabbed hold of Barb's arms and pulled her upwards. The problem was that the heavy folds of satin material kept hooking on the splintered floorboards, making progress slow. Finally, Barb was heaved out, and she lay whimpering on the stage floor, her foot covered in blood.

"We need nurse Sarah!" Billy called.

Mia looked around and was ready to hop on stage and help Billy when Sarah appeared out of nowhere.

"Don't worry, I'll see to it," an out of breath Sarah informed Mia. "You make sure everyone else is okay."

Billy held out a hand and helped Sarah onto the stage. She quickly got to work, dabbing up the blood and bandaging Barb's foot.

"Her ankle is broken," Sarah informed the group. "Move everyone back."

Barb's incessant wailing and gasping made the audience watching below wince. She was obviously in excruciating agony. Maggie used the spectacle as a time to observe the various faces in the crowd. Reginald was pale and his hands were shaking. He looked as though he had seen a ghost.

Pam was making crucifix symbols on her chest with her finger just in case there really was a phantom of the Buttercup Villa theatre. Sylvia's cheeks were wet, a sure sign that she had been crying quietly from the shock.

Maggie turned around and looked at Benedict. He was also pale, and his eyes were serious, as though he had witnessed a murder. One distinctive sign which gave them all away was that their eyes kept darting between each other. Benedict would look at Reggie. Reggie would throw a glance at Sylvia. Sylvia flashed eyes at Benedict, and so the triangle would continue.

"I think it's time," Maggie said, stepping out onto the stage, "that we sort this out once and for all."

All the shocked and pale faces turned to her for answers.

"It was the ghost!" Pam wailed.

"That's what they would like us to believe," Maggie spoke over Pam. "In fact, Pamela, I believe it was your childhood story which provided the inspiration for this whole charade."

Sylvia snorted with laughter. "What are you talking about, old girl? We don't believe in any ghosts."

"Pamela," Maggie addressed her a second time. "Will you come and join us on stage, please?"

Pamela scuttled up the stairs with the help of Billy.

"Would you like to tell everyone gathered here today who you shared the story about the ghost with?"

"Half the town," Pamela laughed.

Maggie closed her eyes momentarily and took a deep breath before opening them. "How about in the last two weeks? Did anyone come for tea, and you told them your childhood memory?"

Pamela scratched at her head. "Ah, yes, how silly of me. I mentioned it to Sylvia. She rarely talks to me, but when I brought that up, she wanted to know everything."

All eyes turned on a scarlet-colored Sylvia who had been slowly backing away to a side exit.

"Not so fast," Maggie instructed. "If you'd like to join us on stage, please, Sylvia. Pamela, thank you for your help."

"I'm alright down here," Sylvia squeaked, but Billy was already at her side to escort her safely up the side stairs.

"Thank you," Maggie said once her furtive friend was standing on stage, working hard not to look at the passed out Barb, or look her friend, Maggie, in the eyes. "Sylvia, dear, would you be so kind as to explain your feelings towards this play?"

Sylvia shifted awkwardly on the spot. "I have no complaints. I think Shakespeare was a really swell guy."

Maggie rolled her eyes. When she opened them the again, Benedict had stepped up.

"If Sylvia will not say anything, I will. I was the one who cut the costumes," Benedict said, raising a guilty hand. "There was no ghost. I just used the story as an excuse to sabotage a few of the costumes. I'm sorry. It was foolish and childish, and I will pay for the damages, Barb."

The audience cried out in disbelief and shock, followed by a wave of intense muttering and gossiping.

"But that's not entirely true, is it?" Maggie interrupted. "You made it perfectly clear that you liked your costume, stockings and all. So, who put you up to it?"

Benedict was fighting with the truth. Maggie admired him for coming forward, but he was not willing to expose the friend he had done it for.

"Here's what I think. Reginald did not want to wear the tights because they were very uncomfortable for his joints. But he knew that if he did any damage, everyone would immediately suspect him, which they did. So Reginald attended his doctor's appointment, ensuring he had an alibi, as he so kindly pointed out to me, and left Benedict to do the dirty deed for him."

Everyone turned and glared at Reginald, who held his hands up in surrender. He dropped his face and stared at the new black slacks he was wearing instead.

"I'm so sorry, Barb," he choked up. "I just didn't want to wear those awfully clothes, but I didn't mean for you to get hurt in any of this."

"What made it a clever crime," Maggie continued, ignoring Reginald's remorse, "was that Benedict needed something done, too."

The audience whispered among themselves.

"What was the one thing Benedict kept complaining about regarding the play?"

"He wanted you as his Juliet!" Mia shouted out loud.

"Excellent, Mia," Maggie approved. "So, who would like to explain what happened next?"

Sylvia stepped forward. Not Reginald. Her cheeks were wet, and she looked thoroughly ashamed of herself.

"I laced some wine with laxatives and gave it to Barb. I thought it would be enough to put her out of action long enough for Maggie to take back the role of Juliet."

"No one would suspect Benedict because the rumor of the ghost had been planted. If Barb took to the stage as Juliet, something bad would happen. Is that why the three of you tried to kill Barb on stage today?"

Sylvia, Benedict, and Reginald all broke out in loud denials that they would do anything so dreadful.

"Well, it was rigged so that Barb would catch fire along with the scripts. And now this. One of you is trying to kill her!" Maggie almost shouted at them.

She wanted the truth, and she was going to pull it out of them.

"No!" Reginald shrieked. "Maggie, please, believe me we never intended to hurt Barb! Yes, I know she is an old cow who bossed us around too much and so I set up a little plan so that the scripts would catch on fire, but I didn't know you'd be the one to get the scripts, Maggie. And I didn't know Barb would wear that ridiculous dress and catch fire! It was Sylvia's idea!"

"Of course it was Sylvia's idea. She hated being told what to do by Barb, so she got you to perform her crime."

All three again exploded with excuses that it was never meant to do anything other than make the play more bearable. No one had intended for Barb to come to lasting harm.

Maggie held up a finger and interrupted them all.

"Excuse me," Maggie said, cutting through the angry voices. "Barb," she gestured to the sleeping woman. "Is quite fine."

Everyone gawked at the heap of unmoving wedding dress on the stage floor. Barb dragged it out a few seconds longer before surprising everyone by sitting upright, wearing a wide lipsticked grin from ear to ear.

There was another unanimous gasp, and Maggie wondered if a murder mystery play would not have gone down better with the locals than their ancient rendition of Romeo and Juliet.

"That means Sarah was in on it too," Benedict pointed out. "I thought I heard a noise under the stage. It must have been Sarah splashing some red dye on Barb's foot."

It impressed Maggie that he was catching on so fast.

"I'm afraid so. She and Billy were the only ones I could trust when all my other friends were in on the crime," Maggie stated dryly, her eyes moving from culprit to culprit. "There's still one unsolved crime. The paint spilled backdrop."

Sylvia, Benedict, and Reggie all eyed each other, passing along silent messages of refute.

"It was not us," Benedict swore.

"I know," Maggie confirmed. "It was the one incident that made little sense. That's when I realized you were committing each other's crimes, except for the one that didn't quite fit in with the others. Besides, I know none of you could climb up to the top of the stage wall. So," Maggie turned to the small sea of faces. "Who dunnit?"

Silence. Followed by a few accusatory stares.

"No one willing to confess? How small in character. Well, I will just have to expose you in front of everyone else -"

"It was me!" Mia blurted. "I'm sorry, okay. I didn't think you would take it so personally."

Maggie hid her surprise. She had been bluffing. She had been so focused on the other crimes that she had no clue who destroyed her backdrop.

"Why?" Billy exploded. "Do you have any idea how many hours Maggie and I spent working on that backdrop together? And you just came along and ruined it!"

"I…" Mia's pink lips flapped noiselessly as words failed her. She blushed deeply and stared at the floor.

"Ahh," Maggie said as the penny dropped. "Perhaps Mia can explain herself to you later, Billy. It may be a little embarrassing for her to do so in front of all these people."

"Look, Maggie, Barb, we're really sorry. We thought it would just be a bit of old fun," Benedict attempted to make light of the situation.

Barb, who had been pulled to her feet, rounded on him.

"Fun?" she barked in his ear. "You people put me through hell. Instead of just manning up and talking to me about the concerns you had."

Maggie raised a finger.

"Yes, Mags darling," Barb allowed the interruption from her new favorite resident.

"I believe the cast members would all agree that they tried to mention a few things to you, Barbara, dear, but you weren't a very good listener," Maggie explained as diplomatically as she could.

There was a chorus of cheering from not only the three culprits, but all the actors, including nurse Mia.

"You had me massage your tired feet for two hours one evening," Mia explained, "even when it was my afternoon off."

"You made me walk to town and order you a cappuccino because the Villa's coffee wasn't 'good enough for a director'," Pam recalled.

"I thought the exercise would do you good," Barb snapped.

"Barb," Maggie spoke with a gentle reprimanding, "I think it's time you explained what's really going on."

Barb absorbed Maggie's words and nodded slowly. She took to center stage, her favored position, and addressed them all with as much humility in her expression as was possible to summon on short notice.

"Maggie attempted to explain to some of you what my problem is a couple of days ago, but it's not her problem to share. I should've told you myself, but I was too proud to admit what was happening. There was a family emergency last month.

"I didn't know you had any living family," Sylvia pointed out, ever suspicious of anything that exited Barb's mouth.

Barb sighed. "I have a daughter. She wants nothing to do with me most of the time, but when she approached me a few months ago, desperate for cash, I gave it to her. That meant," she paced slowly across the stage, taking her time to choose her words, "that I didn't have enough rent money. And then the next month came and, well… you get the pathetic picture that is now me."

"Why not talk to Michelle?" Reginald suggested.

"I did, after all the threatening letters under my door. I tried to come to an arrangement, but it's almost impossible to catch up on what I owe, because my pension remains the same. She gave me one month to come up with a way to bring in money."

"And that's where your awful play came from?" Sylvia realized.

"Exactly. And that's why I turned into a stress-ridden demon who pushed you to inexorable limits. I'm…" she hesitated again, her lips fighting against the words she found so hard to say, "I'm really sorry for my actions and for the stress I've put you under. I will tell Michelle I canceled the play, and I will pack my things and make alternative living arrangements."

With that, Barb, holding her head high, marched backstage and disappeared out the exit before anyone could follow her. Although Maggie, knowing Barb's plan, did, and she offered a tissue to stop the tide of embarrassed tears.

Chapter 12
The Tragedy with a Happy Ending

Maggie watched from behind the curtain as Reginald, acting his second role as Prince, delivered the concluding epilogue to *Romeo and Juliet.*

He stood confidently under the spotlight, his face a mask of utter tragedy as he stared out at the audience and recited:

"'A glooming peace this morning with it brings.

The sun, for sorrow, will not show his head.

Go hence, to have more talk of these sad things.

Some shall be pardoned, and some punished.

For never was a story of more woe

Than this of Juliet and her Romeo."

He then bowed his head. The lights cut, casting the entire hall into absolute darkness. After a few seconds of loaded silence, the audience erupted with loud applause, whistling, and cheering. Backstage they skipped around like children, forgetting for a moment their aching joints and tired muscles.

Barb came round, hugging and kissing each of them.

"I knew you could do it!" Barb whispered in a hoarse voice. She had spent most of the night in the front row mouthing their lines to them. "Thank you for giving me this," she croaked tearfully.

She then ushered them out onto the stage so that the decrepit, limping, and exhausted cast could perform their farewell bow and receive a final round of applause. Barb nearly melted with pride when half the hall climbed to their feet and offered them a standing ovation.

Barb grabbed a microphone and tapped it, signaling to the audience to quiet down.

"Excuse me for interrupting your wonderful applause, but I have to say a few words before you all leave here tonight. As everyone in this cast will know, this play was tough on all of us. Blood, sweat and many tears went into the rehearsals. Being of the older generation, we had a few accidents, a fire or two, and more than one cat fight, but in the end, the residents of Buttercup Villa are more than just a few isolated older folk, we're family. Family with a big heart. So, a special thank you to everyone from Blooming Hill and the surrounding towns who supported us here this evening. And thank you to all the cast members who worked along with me to produce something we could only dream we could do this far along in our lives. And one last mention of Ms.

Maggie Belle. Without her, none of this would've taken place."

The hall filled with happy cheers and clapping again. Maggie caught sight of Michelle Pier, the fiery owner of Buttercup Villa, hovering on the side of the stage and clearly hoping for an invitation to join them, but none such was given.

Benedict broke away from Maggie's side and made his way to the front. He took the microphone from Barb's hand and addressed the audience with a wide smile.

"Good evening, ladies and gentleman," Benedict began.

He had to wait for much of the women in the audience to die down before he continued.

"On behalf of the cast, and the town, we would like to hand over a rather generous gift to the director and producer of this performance. Barb Bristle, would you please accept this?" Benedict waited as Billy ran over with a bouquet of roses and a small envelope, which was at least an inch thick. "You deserve this, after everything we've put you through."

After a lot more cheering and a blur of congratulations, Maggie could finally break away from the crowd and find a peaceful corner to catch her breath. She thought of the events a mere two days before, with Barb cancelling the play and storming off stage.

It had not been hard to convince the cast to perform anyway, especially after they knew of Barb's financial situation. Ticket sales had more than covered Barb's debt, according to Sarah, and provided enough to paint the villa's old roof. But Benedict's public, yet secret, apology at the end with the wad of cash had been his own doing. She had to admit that she had been quite wrong about Benedict's character.

She had readily dismissed him as being flirty, ostentatious, and shallow, and yet he kept surprising her with a deeper version of himself that he rarely allowed anyone else to see. He was certainly flawed, but so was she.

"Barb's not the only one I bought flowers for," Benedict's voice found her lost in thought. "How could I not give my fair Juliet a bouquet too? Thank you for performing alongside me this evening. I know I'm certainly not your choice in Romeo, but it was a privilege for me to at least pretend we were 'star-crossed lovers' for a night."

Maggie smiled and hated herself for blushing. She had never imagined that after more than a decade of losing her husband, and being in her sixties, that she would ever experience the tingle of emotion wreaking havoc inside her stomach. She was not some giddy teenager who could not reign in her emotions, and yet she hung onto Benedict's every word.

"It was rather kind of you to make it up to Barb the way you did."

"We were wrong to put Barb through what we did. Even worse, we were wrong to exclude you from our idiotic plans. Perhaps if we had let you in sooner, you could have reasoned us out of our madness."

Maggie chuckled. "Friends?"

"Yes, please," Benedict implored, extending a hand to take hers.

Maggie felt someone else watching them. She heard a man clear his throat, and she turned to find Sarah, one kid on her hip and the other holding her hand, standing next to her father. Sheriff Cedric Duncan was in a normal suit, sans the police badge, and was holding an enormous bouquet of deep red roses.

Sarah waited for her father to speak, but Cedric was at a loss for words.

"Uhm, Dad said he really enjoyed your performance, didn't you, Dad?" Sarah began, hoping to kick-start her father.

"Uh… yes… yes. You were an excellent Juliet. Not a word out of place in all those lines," Cedric continued, his eyes watching Maggie. "I brought you these…" he stooped and awkwardly thrust the roses at Maggie. He paused halfway when he realized she was already holding a bouquet.

"Thank you, Sheriff," Maggie said politely, though she was drenched in sweat and quite panicked. "I can never have too many flowers."

"You were both wonderful," Sarah gushed. She gave them each a peck on the cheek. "Well, we'd better be going. Oh, Benedict, Max sent over flowers. Well, there was no tag, but I assumed they were from him apologizing."

"Excellent," Benedict replied with a smile, though to Maggie it looked as though he had the wind knocked out of his sails.

"Right, well, bye then!" Sarah waved and walked off with her father, who cast one last glance over his shoulder at Maggie.

"Seems like the sheriff fancies you," Benedict stated with a weak smile. "And his flowers are far more worthy. Perfect roses from a shop. I just collected mine from the courtyard garden."

Maggie looked down and realized the difference in bouquets, her eyes straying to Benedict's colorful one.

"That's alright, Mr. Benedict," Billy said, walking over with a wide grin. "Maggie told me she chose her husband because he picked her field flowers instead of one of the stuffy bouquets from the shop."

Billy handed over a posy of daisies. "You were brilliant tonight. Only you could figure everyone out and make them smile at each other again after such a dreadful war."

"You give me too much credit," Maggie laughed. "Did Mia ever come and talk to you?"

"Nope." Billy shook his head.

"So, you haven't figured out why she sabotaged the backdrop?" Benedict asked, with a twinkle in his eye.

Billy frowned. "Should I have?"

Maggie sighed and shook her head. "Perhaps you should dig less and look around you more."

"I'm totally lost, Ms. Maggie," Billy admitted.

"Mia likes you," Benedict blurted. "Haven't you noticed how she's always trying to be around you?"

Billy frowned while he thought back. Clearly, he had not.

"Mia destroyed the backdrop because she was jealous of the time we were spending together. Believe it or not, she's jealous of our friendship. She wanted you to notice her for a change," Maggie explained in a low voice so that no one else would pass by and overhear.

"She likes me!" Billy scoffed. "That's ridiculous."

Maggie hid her surprise. "I thought you might like her, too. You mentioned having your eye on someone, and I just assumed it was her."

Billy laughed loudly, his laugh both a mixture of the boy he was at heart and the man he had become on the outside.

"I do like someone, but it's not Mia. She's too self-absorbed for me. I told you the woman I like loves to help other people," Billy reminded her.

"Old boy, if you're after our Maggie, you've got to get in line," Benedict informed him. "Sheriff's up first."

Billy's face drained of color. "No, no... well, my girl is a little older than me, but sorry, Ms. Maggie, you're out of my league, in more than one way."

"I totally agree," Maggie laughed.

"But don't worry, I've made my first move," Billy explained. "I sent her a bunch of flowers. Anonymous of course. Anyway, I need to catch my lift home. See you tomorrow."

They watched in silence as Billy ran off and back into the busy hall.

"That can't be coincidence, right?" Benedict broke the quiet.

"No, I don't think it is. I think our young man believes himself in love with Sarah Duncan," Maggie explained.

"Who would've thought a play filled with such tragedy and death could ignite the hope of love in so many people?" Benedict observed.

Maggie was studying the two bouquets in her arms, remembering fondly the wild field flowers which had looked so similar to the ones Benedict had picked for her.

"Who indeed," she replied with a smile playing across her lips.

The End

Now that you have finished this cozy mystery, please consider posting a review on Amazon. It would be appreciated.